WOO WOO

the posthumous love story of

Miss Emily Carr

WOO WOO

the posthumous love story of
Miss Emily Carr

Veronica Knox

silent

PUBLISHING

Library and Archives Canada Cataloguing in Publication
Knox, Veronica, 1949-
Woo Woo: the posthumous love story of Miss Emily Carr / Veronica Knox.

ISBN 978-0-9877415-1-6

1. Carr, Emily, 1871-1945--Fiction. I. Title.

PS8621.N695W66 2012 C813'.6 C2012-906909-4

Editor: Linda Clement
Cover design: Iryna Spica & Veronica Knox
Text formatting: Spica Book Design

Cover photograph is a composite collage of two separate images:
Head – *Emily Carr,* from photograph I-60892, courtesy of Royal BC Museum, BC Archives
Body – *The Bride* – Julia Margaret Cameron, from the Royal Photographic Society collection, public domain

Second Edition

Printed and bound in Canada
by Printorium Bookworks, Victoria B.C.

Silent K Publishing:
Victoria, British Columbia

www.woowoothenovel.com
www.veronicaknox.com
email: veronica@veronicaknox.com

10 9 8 7 6 5 4 3 2

- for Sarah and David -

There's no time like the past to start again

Table of Contents

Preface

Painter and author, Emily Carr (1871 – 1945) was the honorary eighth member of the Canadian artists known as the 'Group of Seven'. Her paintings have become the definitive portrait of the Canadian West and a tribute to her studies abroad of the impressionist movement.

As a young woman, Emily braved a solo expedition to a string of remote First Nations settlements of British Columbia. Her on-site illustrations of neglected totem poles disintegrating in decimated villages helped to document a fast-disappearing culture. When she was twenty-seven, she was given the native name 'Klee Wyck, the laughing one'.

Emily became an eccentric icon of her hometown Victoria, on Vancouver Island. She was frequently seen in her later years, a dowdy plump old bird pushing a baby's pram filled with pottery clay or groceries, accompanied by a tangle of the Griffon dogs she bred, and Woo, a Java monkey that perched on her shoulder, wearing a dress.

Emily eventually became famous for her curmudgeon ways, but she flaunted the rules of society at an early age. Something untoward in her teenage years caused her to reject the intimate loves of her life. One suitor in particular, pursued Emily to the end of her days.

Much local conjecture surrounds the hints of Emily's lost love in her books as well as her letters and diaries.

Today, an historic mystery man continues to hover over Emily Carr's memoirs like a ghost.

Emily Carr
1871-1945

Last night I was on my way to 'the place' again.
How strange that I am so often conscious of that place.
It is very familiar, but where is it? I am never quite there.
I look up at it and down on it
and on the way I know the country all about it,
but actually I never enter the estate.
I wonder if I ever shall.

~ Emily Carr ~
Hundreds and Thousands
1938

Don't pickle me away as a done.

~ Emily Carr ~

Emily Regrets

n retrospect, it probably wasn't wise to give a monkey the wedding rings. But, it was a surreal sight watching Woo hop towards the bride and groom balancing a silk pillow in one hand, and not much of a surprise when the ceremony disintegrated into farce. Trained animals rarely fail to disappoint at the optimum moment.

It was barely three weeks ago, on the last day of September, that I had the first inkling that I may have lost my mind mere days after I lost my heart. I was three kilometers outside the celebrated James Bay 'Carr Triangle' of Victoria on Vancouver Island – the old homestead of Miss Emily Carr, renowned international artist and iconic curmudgeon. It was my last stop on an interrupted tour – a small square footage of forever. Emily's final resting place. That was the week after I became a princess.

"I was seventeen when I had my first heart attack. It took three more to actually kill me."

These were the disembodied words I heard that changed my life and my capacity for rational thought.

I checked the date on my rolled up *Times-Colonist*. It was still 2012. The female voice declared itself to be a woman named Emily. It was no stretch to add the surname Carr, considering I was standing over her grave at the time.

I am twenty-seven-years-old, still an artist in search of everything and I declare so with pride. I am a freelance historian. Research is a rich field of dreams, and I paint as often as I can between the assignments that keep me sequestered in the rich archives of British Columbia.

A year ago, I was newly arrived in Victoria: fresh from graduation with a master's degree in Fine Arts from the University of Alberta, where an instructor had told me that one of my paintings reminded him of the work of Emily Carr. I checked and he was wrong, but I was flattered.

I didn't fully appreciate Van Gogh until after Emily softened the path to the French Impressionists. Emily's work was my Rosetta Stone for reading the earlier iconographic provenance of the debauched club of absinthe-soaked Old Boys, who had painted from the downtown brothels of feral Paris. I have long been grateful to her for that.

I resumed my painting techniques with a more exotic palette. Sure enough, Emily gave me the insight to experience emotional light. She slapped me black and blue with her colours. I felt indebted.

Subsequently, my affinity for Emily's style, led me to daydream that I may be Emily Carr reincarnated. I mean, I *am* a painter and writer, I *was* bitten by a monkey, and I've had *two* Old-English sheepdogs. What more evidence could there be?

Woo Woo   VERONICA KNOX

Of course, a great deal more.

Reincarnation is a ridiculous leftover notion from my mother's New-Age books of the sixties. I am the next generation, and I have grown-up to realize metaphysics is all rot. Besides, hiking in the wilderness is not even on my list of things I like to do, and I hate any form of camping.

After I moved to Victoria, I traipsed the expected Emily tourist-routes: I checked out the city's art gallery, the museums, and Carr House, and poked around Emily's old neighbourhood. I saved visiting her burial place for last, but circumstances delayed paying tribute, so it was a year later when I finally made the pilgrimage and trod the gravel path to her grave. I was loaded down with a sketchbook and camera, pens and wax crayons, a roll of tissue paper, chocolate, newspaper, a potted plant of wild heartsease, and a feeling of reverent expectation.

Before I set off for the cemetery, I had a visitation from my romantic muse – an optimist, who writes fluent gibberish in flowery handwriting most unlike my own. It began as usual, with its melodramatic accent: *the startling thrill is imminent. I am ready to face death – absorbing the immortal presence of the great sharing. Today I remain open and receptive to the world of shadows.* After that it rambled for two whole pages about flowers and birds that, even now, escapes translation, but it served to inspire my trek. I savored the moment, devoting an entire afternoon to my expedition – to fancifully commune with Miss Emily Carr.

Scholars call ancient languages dead, but I was

about to experience the absence of life and poetry would turn out to have little to do with it.

I had envisioned the Ross Bay Cemetery as a formal gated community with a tree-lined approach that purposely and elegantly muffled the business of life, but a main road had been permitted to roar, invasively parallel to the assigned resting place of Victoria's fragile ex-citizens.

Undaunted, I closed my eyes and chose a direction to the left of the main entrance, sending a fanciful greeting ahead of me to the memory of Emily: "It's me Emily, where are you?"

I tramped and missed, determined to find Emily by some internal dowsing rod. Logic told me to scan for an impressive monument, and by doing so, I passed her by several times. I was growing irritable. My feet ached, I was starving, the sky had darkened, and I became increasingly unimpressed with my intuition. I finally had to consult a map posted on the caretaker's shack, and almost gave up. The diagram placed her in the U-shaped sector for Presbyterians, number 15 on the scale of descending points of interest.

I retraced my steps on a patchwork path between the graves to Emily's side, picking my way through a crazy-quilt landscape of haphazard stone squares and rectangles, and finally stared down at a bleak plot of low-lying real estate, designated H85E15. No great marble obelisk rose above her, and she was a matter of yards away from the heaviest road traffic.

No doubt, if such a thing exists, patriarch Richard Carr was turning in his grave over an intrusion worse than the brothel which had polluted his once pristine (Carr-controlled) neighborhood. If nothing else, the name Fairfield Road, named for its original fairground, was quintessential irony. Gasoline fumes and dust polluted the air. A pastoral paradise on fair ground it was not.

My first impression was denial. I had been shocked at the lack of a civic monument considering Emily's contribution to the culture and tourism of the area. At least, a marble sheepdog for loyalty I thought, or a miniature totem pole, or a bronze monkey in a dress. But no. All there was here, was a token flat plate in the ground void of organic sentiment, and a low crude stump of concrete offering Emily's grim statement of wanting to be buried sans coffin, rather than one of her snappier upbeat quotes.

The latest Carr House is a raised plinth-affair like a box garden gone to seed. According to the placement of her bronze plaque, Emily is crammed against the upper left-hand corner under a tangle of tawny thatch grass. There was a motley assortment of extraordinarily-grotesque pottery colored with neon markers which, ironically, made Emily's own ersatz First Nations-ware look like great art. Even Emily admitted her little cottage-industry venture of native souvenirs was a shameless imitation for tourist's small-change.

I felt the urge to go home and fill a vase with a bright bouquet of used long-stemmed paintbrushes for her. Instead, I placed the plain white planter of growing heartsease I had brought. It was the most appropriate sign of life I could leave behind to symbolize what I thought of cemeteries in general.

Emily' perfunctory *fan mail* of crude offerings looked like junk from a garage sale and reminded me of Jim Morrison's infamous Père Lachaise grave statue in Paris, graffiti'd in careless celebration of a creative life. In memoriam, not. His defaced bust (based on a likeness of Alexander the Great) was eventually stolen, but at least rock-star Jim once had a monument worth more than the price of a disposable camera. His tortured greatness had been commemorated by art, and in comparison, Emily's art had been down-played.

While it's true, that elsewhere in public places, Emily is celebrated in fine murals and bronze, here on her quintessential memorial spot, visited by hundreds of tourists, was a poor show of cursory anticlimactic sentiment.

I heard the chattering of a squirrel in the cedar branches above as I sat on the edge of the significantly - *dead* grass, and toasted Emily with warm ginger-ale. I wrote in my journal:

> *Dear Em – Your death sucks. Your love-life lacks closure. Is this all there is? A damp house filled with estranged relics, a once-pastoral neighborhood choked with hot real estate, and a patch of dried grass? At least art lives on, honored beyond the human disintegration of muscle and bone. How unfair. Consider yourself lucky to have missed the devolution.*
>
> *Who is your mystery man? I'm dying to know. You are not here.*

Woo Woo   VERONICA KNOX

"Say hi to Vincent for me," I said to the creaking wind hovering over the spot where I guessed Emily's head might be. I assumed the casket had been correctly oriented, as if putting the deceased to bed (the marker, being the headboard) but it was impossible to be sure.

I sketched the unkempt grave, noting the bleak inscription: *artist and author – lover of nature*. Accurate as may be, but decidedly Spartan. I put my tissue paper and wax crayons away, unused. The words were not worth the effort of a brass rubbing. "I'm bored to death," I said out loud to the ground and added, "no disrespect intended."

That's when I heard the voice declaring itself to be Emily. It was a non-threatening statement delivered in a stage-whisper, and I captured it in a scribble by force of habit, thinking it was my fanciful imagination. My mind is always working, especially when I'm adrift on free time. People call it being lost in thought: I call it finding a *missing* thought. Duly recorded, I closed my notebook. Other than the voice, it had been a dull afternoon, but the sky had darkened and threatened rain, and I was out of chocolate.

Perception, intuitive hunches, and an insatiable curiosity, are the creative elements I bring to my professional game. I consider it smart business practice to run a permanently-receptive program, dialled to bloodhound mode, and like any reporter, I jot at opportune moments. Fleeting memos tend to retreat until anchored in stone or chiselled in ballpoint.

I constantly add to my growing Emily file, and I was particularly intrigued with everything paranormal at the moment. I had been softly debating ghosts for weeks with Jon. Real ones, not the elusive bits of data I refer to as literary ghosts, but then I speak for the skeptical side.

Being the star of Victoria, Emily was a regular subject of the queries that cluttered my in-basket. Wild theories collect around her cautious diaries, but I am a fact-finder. I stand firm behind science-non-fiction *over* the human need to embellish stories. Facts need a safe place to land, but I have a whimsical side and in a romantic moment I wrote this Haiku:

meaningful nothings
day in, day out
stars fall on paper

It's a somewhat futile gesture to stand, lording it over death, trying to bond with bones – the last resort for a fan seeking a celebrity rush. These are the places we can be sure our heroes will always be, in the secret gloat of their private hereafter. We can visit them to rub shoulders and hope that something rises. We have them cornered. We stand six feet above fame, alone with an elite species; if we are moved at all, we leave sobered by the immensities and trivialities of life and death. It's a sombre thought, that leaving one's flesh is called the *after*-life for a reason.

Standing quietly in the deepest reveries of communion, we can sometimes be transported internally from the sheer awe of being in the precise

WooWoo VERONICA KNOX

longitude and latitude of greatness – a place these icons never were in life.

With Emily, it was different: hers was a family plot, and she had stood here as parents and siblings had been interred, perhaps even shivered to realize she too would take the same carriage ride in a box to this very address.

She may have foreseen her own post mortem procession: slipping silently down Government Street to Humboldt after crossing Douglas, and passing the Episcopal Reformed Church of her childhood, moving slowly in homage to Saint Ann's old convent, and Saint Joseph's hospital where sister Lizzie died, and finally wending up Fairfield to the eternal embrace of Ross Bay – a misnomer of ironic proportions. No fair field in sight. Just an overgrown landscape of low grey shapes causing the wind to whistle as it traveled west to the open sea, moaning through the straggle of interrupted dreams, and playing lonely tunes on the uneven rows of chewed bleached stones. Poetic indeed.

I couldn't stay long. Out of civic duty, I had left Jenner, my Irish Wolfhound, in the car with the windows rolled down as far as I dared. In a visit to Scotland's million old churches, I had seen notices posted at every lych-gate barring the presence of canines, with or without owners. Cats were free to prowl uninterrupted, and even added to the ambiance of the macabre, but dogs were high maintenance and left more high-profile *footprints*. Felines at least, had the dignity to bury their leavings like small coffins.

Judging by the past historic abuses of the original Pioneer cemetery downtown, and the number of bag-free dog walkers in the Dallas Road off-leash park, it was unlikely anyone would care if a mongrel defiled an acre of uninspired horticulture such as this, but I take the responsibilities of dog ownership seriously.

Before I returned to the incarcerated Jenner, I snapped a few pictures of the less famous, but more thoughtful, markers the graveyard had to offer: the 'Pooley Angel', with traces of red vandalism still in its crevices; a miniature stone armchair holding a pair of petrified baby's booties, and a fireman's helmet that looked like a lava-coated relic from Pompeii.

It started to rain, and I began to crave Jasmine tea and Chicken Korma with sliced almonds and chutney, in an obscenely ravenous way. Hunger got me out of there before the deluge.

It was a morbid thought of mis-orientation which toyed with my brain on the drive home: a coffin twists and turns in its trajectory from undertaker to graveside, and being unadorned and symmetrical (unless there's a plaque on its lid) how would anyone know which way around the body lay? It brought weird thoughts of an obscure mortician's rune – a quick hieroglyph at one end of the casket before the lid closed that rubbed off with a quick polish at the last minute, like the chalk marks the parking meter squad leaves on one's *car* tires.

The depressing possibility of two cryptic plaques, one atop the other, was sadly uncreative to venerate an intrepid artist like Emily, and I had declared as much out loud to the bereft, overcast afternoon. Remorse spattered my windshield and

Woo Woo

ran like greasy tears dripping down my car's face –
down Emily Carr's face.

I drove on, even more committed to the prospect
of one day being an urn of ashes tipped into the
breeze on a spring morning.

When I got home, via the curry house from hell,
I headed for the teapot and dog treats, and added a notation about the word 'incarcerated' in my
journal, separating the words *in* and *car* and sup-
planting the word *Carr* and *care*. I wrote the word
superficial and underlined it in red. The word 'car'
dared me at every turn.

I reread the words I had heard: *my name is Emily.
I was seventeen when I had my first heart attack. It
took three more to actually kill me.*

I was sure if I stared at it long enough a subliminal gem would reveal itself.

I love the occult messages that lurk within languages like the perfect Victorian child, to be seen
and not heard.

The first graves
in Ross Bay Cemetery
looked very lonely and far apart
because Episcopalians could not
lie beside Nonconformists,
nor could Catholics rest beside Episcopalians.
Methodists, Chinese, and paupers buried by the city
and people who believed in nothing at all,
had to lie, each in a separate part of the cemetery.
But, the waves of Ross Bay
boomed against the cemetery bank and broke it.
They bit into the earth, trying to wash out the coffins.
They seemed to say,
I, the sea, can take better care of you,
the dead, than the earth can.
My gulls will cry over all of you alike.
In me, all denominations
can mingle.

~ Emily Carr ~
The Book of Small

Something seems to keep you out,
I don't know what,
a certain private feel, not law but delicacy.
I wonder where this place is.

~ Emily Carr ~
Hundreds and Thousands
1937

Scottie

My name is Alba Watson, but everyone calls me Scottie. I will probably never eat Indian takeout again, and I am all too familiar with the obscure landscape Emily refers to, I've glimpsed it all my life. *This* life, not a past one. Let me be clear about that.

I collect data in several places, but my office is at home in an eclectic living room under one of my own paintings of a large purple, green, and blue tiger. Part of my workweek is spent in the downtown branch of the public library and the museum annex on Belleville Street, which houses the Archives of British Columbia.

Both are microfilm worlds, where news spins by one's nose in a stream of blurred text and squares of history. Islands of copy and photographs break the monotony of a long and straight grey read.

Happily, the greater part of modern research is accessed by personal computer – an online world where I scan for road signs, staring slightly out of focus, foraging for bold headlines that point the way to my elusive destination, the lost city of Eureka.

When the occasion calls, I can be found ferreting in another vault of trivia in the private attics and catacombs of Victoria. When I relax, it's to read or paint or to peck over the skeleton of a mystery novel.

If I can't sleep, I indulge in the luxury of a bed-time story, read aloud. Audio books are the greatest invention since librarians. Although the story should be engaging, it's always the voice that carries the magic. A narrator who plays the words like music and acts between the lines is required.

The fluid rhythms of the theatre are rare. Children's books are my first choice, as they are meant to be told with the traditional fireside storyteller's captivating opening: *Are you listening? Then I shall begin.*

My favorite is *Harry Potter* – the English version, read by Stephen Fry. Stephen reads and I'm there. It's no surprise I have so many dreams about *Hogwarts & Co.* Stephen's *Harry* is my sedative. I drowse and float off in the first chapter on intonations softer than a feather bed. Which I suppose is the point; sound sleep is magic within the coziness a good B&B... bed and blankets.

The happiest perk of working from home is that Jenner isn't left alone all day. He and I walk the short distance to Beacon Hill Park during my lunch hour and stretch our six legs in a few circuits around the grounds of St. Ann's Academy on the way home. We live across the street in a unique building converted from a hospital to a labyrinth of pet-friendly apartments.

Jenner is a rescue dog, and I had needed rescuing. Physical proof of my existence had been fast becoming a rumor. He keeps me exercised and leads me faithfully into the airs above ground. If it weren't for Jenner, I would be in danger of becoming an Egyptian mummy, buried under a ton of papyrus. Lucky for me, I love the smell and sound of history and the sublime aura of shy knowledge hidden between the pages of a book. It's the electronic delving which exhausts me. Fortunately, books are not yet obsolete, and much of what I am asked to locate is locked in the musty habitats of academia. Solitude is my country of choice. The world 'upstairs & social' had not been for me. If anyone had commented on my predominantly-internalized world, I would have quipped: "My dance card is perfectly full thank you, very much."

Some days I don't know if my name is Watson or Sherlock or Nancy Drew, but I do know that I didn't use to believe in ghosts or channeling the dead. I thought I never would accept such a thing, but now I'm beginning to understand the latter with a dash of scientific perspective.

No séance rooms and table-rapping for me. I put my recent encounter down to kindred thoughts, the collective unconscious, and genetic memories, but there are hints of more. My boyfriend Jon says there's more. I fell in love with him on a Friday although we never met till the following Sunday.

Jon is an amateur paranormal investigator, writer of non-fiction, and practiced etymologist. His daily life is spent as a marine biologist. I kid him that he's a ghostwriter, but Jon loves the title because he's a wordsmith. We both love words: plays on words, audio words, visual words, anagrams, word associations, and the subtle nuances of spelling that flirt with rhythm, and pronunciation.

I first indulged Jon's supernatural theories because he had enchanted my brain, but soon after we met, circumstances permitted me to accept his hypothesis not only as possible, but irrefutable evidence.

At the time it seemed several coincidences joined us at the crossroads of synchronicity and inevitability. The laws of psychic magnetism had been a ridiculous notion to me, premising ethereal vibrations and karma had drawn us together. I think the exact place we met was *where the hell have you been?*

Jon used to be my client. He engaged me as a research assistant for twenty-four hours, and then we began researching each other.

Not long after that, a bizarre encounter ripped the fabric of our personal universe to shreds. Jon said it had been about time.

It's complicated.

Are you listening? Then I shall begin.

It was the cows who laid out the town...
...cow hooves hardened the mud into twisty lanes...
...people just followed in the cow's footsteps.

~ Emily Carr ~
The Book of Small

Me & M.E.

had tried with some difficulty, to erase the jumble of a hundred-and-fifty years of real estate in order to see the original street plan when Victoria was young and James Bay had been a few farms compatibly nestled against Beacon Hill Park.

In 1864, the site of Carr House was still considered a few miles from the town – a deceiving distance because it's only a four block stroll to the busy inner harbour which is considered the heart of Victoria.

But this is the challenge of the historian who must isolate the present in order to read the past. I had held two maps, wishing I was a bird. Only a bird could rise above the one way street confusion and the snarl of traffic and appreciate the juxtaposition of Carr House with two other properties, once on the same parcel of land, connected by three spinster sisters – the elderly Miss Carrs.

I was not much different than an archaeologist hacking through a dense jungle to find a lost temple where a civilization began, but due to legal property lines, the laws of trespassing, and the rights of privacy, it was harder. An 'as the crow flies' trek is now an impossibility, and aerial photographs are the only way to appreciate the scale of the original colony.

It's important to visualize the lay of the land to understand the idyllic life of the imaginative child, 'Millie', who once ruled these parts which was, in her time, a kingdom and she the youngest and fairest princess of the king and queen.

The quintessential life of Emily Carr began as a fairy tale in a garden of make-believe amongst the intoxicating scents of pine and cedar, the heady fragrances of wildflowers, and the perfume of cultivated roses.

Emily was fortunate to be born a child of privilege during the transplanting of ye olde English society to the new world. She sprang from a pair of wealthy genteel settlers who staked out new lives in the frontier of western Canada during a wave of colonization.

Emily was born in 1871 during the transitional growth of the city named for Queen Victoria. Her father, Richard Carr, was one of the many successful entrepreneurs who established thriving businesses, but Emily also grew up amongst a ragtag populace of working-class servants, pioneers, soldiers, prospectors, natives, impoverished immigrants, and misfits, who helped define a unique offshoot of British culture in a clearing of North American primeval rainforest.

As a curious child, 'Millie' observed the dynamics of power through witnessing the contrasts of hardship and favour first hand. She admired the grit of the First Nation people and noted the status

Woo Woo   VERONICA KNOX

and poverty they shared with the Chinese immigrants imported for hard labour.

Brothels and saloons operated in close proximity to the formal garden parties of the newly transplanted gentility. One such establishment had even compromised the Carr's pocket of paradise after Father Carr naively sold a small portion of his land to a speculator. Thereafter, the family's tranquility was forever thwarted by an obnoxious presence adjoining their property. Social lines were drawn early to delineate the garden acreages of the upper-class citizenry and the uneducated cultures ostracized in segregated ghettos and settlements, as well as those less fortunate who lived on the first streets that sprouted on the reclaimed mudflats of the harbour. M.E. 'Millie-Emily' crossed them all.

Poetry was pure joy,
love more than half pain.

~ Emily Carr ~
Growing Pains

Headline Interrupt-Us

*J*on's first phone call intruded at 4:55 pm on an unsuspecting Friday afternoon as I was getting ready to take Jenner for a walk. His voice got straight to the point. "Miss Watson, my name is Jon Locke, thank you for taking my call at such an unprofessional hour. Please don't go home."

It was a compelling intro. I pushed back the sleeve of my lucky blue sweater to check my wristwatch, only to find a band of pale skin where it used to be.

"That's okay, I *am* home," I said, "but I was about to head out."

"I have an odd request," the voice went on.

"Go ahead," I said, and continued to search the desk and floor for my favorite wavy-shaped Salvador Dali watch, silently chiding myself for not having its wonky buckle repaired.

Jon's voice on speakerphone made him sound as though he were from another dimension. "I'm putting together a last minute presentation concerning a haunted tennis court in Rocklands, and I need your help tracing the owners of the property. Are you able to oblige? It's time-sensitive. My deadline is Monday morning. Please say yes."

Woo Woo VERONICA KNOX

Jenner sniffed the phone and whined. That noise we humans like to think is doggy sadness. I was fairly distracted by my lost watch – only half paying attention to my caller, searching for the melting clock face from Dali's 'the Persistence of Memory'. Ironically for the moment, time felt distorted. "No time to lose," I said, referring to my mood.

"None at all," came the reply.

"Isn't it a bit ironic to have a *dead*line for a ghost story?" I asked, still rummaging.

"It's more of a business deal."

"With a tennis-playing spectre?"

"No, I think the woman spirit is the wife of the first owner. It's a private residence. A friend of mine is a realtor. He has a sale pending if he can report the juiciest history of the house. The prospective buyer has been actively seeking a century house with a ghost. I'm involved because this is my field of interest, and the project came to me out of the blue. I trust those. Don't you?"

"Depends on the shade of blue," I answered, studying my sky-blue sleeve.

I let the voice continue to plead its case for my weekend. My watch was either here or not. Before I engaged the speakerphone an attached cord had made me the prisoner of a limited search radius, but even afterwards there was only a narrow zone of investigation open to me.

I comforted myself that there was a good chance my watch would be in the car and not in the library's lost and found drawer, or worse, outside on the pavement at the mercy of any old passerby and the weather. For sure it was going to upset me until it was found. The loss of a ring years ago still bothered me. Colleagues said I had a tidy mind.

I continued to sift the contents of my purse and briefcase as Jon expounded upon the magnitude of his dilemma. Both carryalls revealed mounds of dead receipts and extinct shopping lists, and I took the opportunity to spring clean the accumulation of several weeks worth of life's detritus.

I had never understood how a man could function without the 'bag of convenience' we women lug everywhere, until I researched a paper for a visiting anthropology professor, and learned we are a race of hunters and gatherers, and that it was the women who were the dominant providers. Male Cro Magnons protected the homes that their women filled with *stuff*. Our portable knapsacks evolved from the first shopping carts that held every edible berry and nut, and interesting rock and twig, which may prove useful back in the cave. Mine was a veritable magnet for coins, pens, and an overabundance of personal grooming supplies. But, sadly, no Dali watch.

I tried to give the call my full attention: Jon was outlining his details. "I need names and photographs that will hopefully match the descriptions of the eyewitnesses for the meeting, Monday," he said.

I paused, leaned into the telephone dial, and spoke more directly. "You're meeting with a ghost, a realtor, *and* a buyer?"

"And a psychic, yes."

"And this isn't a joke?

"Miss Watson, it's too absurd to be a joke. I've been hired as the voice of science in a sticky situation where at least five people are desperate for justice."

"You sound more like a lawyer for the deceased."

"I am on their side. *Possession* of a home runs deep."

I gave up on my watch and eased into my chair. "So, a scientist by day and a supernatural hero by night?" I countered, and shut off the speaker mode.

Jon's voice came into focus and resonated with a pleasant shock in my left ear. I paid more attention, and Jenner shape-shifted to a slump of grey fur at my feet.

"Marine biologist," I heard him say, "I'm a marine biologist by day *and* by night. I've dabbled in paranormal investigation since I met a ghost when I was ten. For me, it's a commitment. I made a promise."

"To a ghost?" I said, reaching for a notepad and an assortment of coloured pens.

"I pride myself on having an open mind," he said. "I dislike using the word dabble when it refers to phenomena of a paranormal nature. I assure you, I am always the voice of discretion." He hesitated a nanosecond and added, "I have to be, my credibility depends on it."

I listened more carefully. "You're a skeptic then?" I stared at a patch of missing wallpaper on the wall across the room and decided its shape failed as an Rorschach inkblot test scanning for psychological life.

"No, I'm a believer, but most phenomena of this nature is ruled out as something natural. I am a scientist, first and forever. Pseudoscience is for the movies."

My voice change to a more receptive tone, "I am relieved to hear it," I said.

His voice turned hopeful, "there's still time to negotiate a reasonable offer."

"It's a little too late for reason, I think, but..."

"Miss Watson..."

"Alba. Call me Alba."

"Alba. It may be the late, and so-far benign, Mrs. Ghostbody, of an extremely *fixed* abode, who deserves a fair deal. Her home is on the block, yet again. The present owners are desperate to be away after taking drastic steps to exorcize their investment, and, unbelievably, they've drawn the perfect buyer who wants a property with verifiable paranormal activity. But the communication has to be positive, interactive, and friendly. Which is where I come in. My realtor friend wants to close, and, if all parties are satisfied, I will have mediated a situation out of the twilight zone, and hopefully healed a rift of some lasting emotional upheaval. Are those reason enough?"

He took a long breath, and I heard him rustle his own papers, presumably on a desk as creaking with work as mine. His inflections told as much as his words. "I will also have obtained more authenticated research for the study I'm conducting about local *haunted* houses. Sorry, I hate that word too, but it cuts to the chase. Victoria is an extremely *active* city."

"I sympathize with your predicament, and when you put it like that, it does take on a noble cause. I can understand, that you're in a paranormal pickle, and while I don't guarantee juice on such short notice, I could collect some basic facts, but I would have to insist that my name not be credited. I have a reputation to keep as well."

"Understood. You come highly recommended, which is why I called you. That word 'could' gives me hope."

"You mean it wasn't that other resources had closed shop for the day?"

"Alba, I don't believe in luck. I was in need of a research expert. You answered my call. Likely, it was for an obscure reason neither of us will ever know, but leaving that aside, I sense you are intrigued."

I glanced down at my handiwork between pen and the phone. I had drawn a green tree with a red sun impaled on one of its branches, a large black capital M with flourishes, and blue parallel wavy lines in the background that connected them together like sound waves.

It was my turn to deliver a surprise."I think I met a ghost when I was a kid, too. I just refused to accept it."

"Why would you do that? It's such a privilege. You were chosen, Alba Watson."

I hesitated. "Because," I said, "my ghost was a monkey."

The silence was more like static. I barely had the time to exhale before Jon indicated he considered my personal confession to be a bonus. I heard the smile in his voice when he called it much 'anticipated fodder' for his own research.

Jenner's bark was sharp. One quick, impatient yipe reminded me it was time for his walk. I was swamped with work and about to decline diplomatically, though I was intrigued as the voice so correctly intuited, so I was surprised to hear my voice say, "What have you got for me?" as I fired up my computer, still warm from Friday-business.

There was a sigh of relief from the receiver, "an address, some audio clues: the sounds of a tennis match and a disembodied scorekeeper, a misty blob on a phone camera, and several reports from eye-witnesses. I'm tracking them down as we speak. I'll interview them and cross-reference their stories with what you find. I need any corroborating news-paper reports of sightings, and as I mentioned, an up-to-date provenance of the building and site. Are you going to save me?"

"Synchronize watches," I announced, and he laughed. I frowned; I had no watch to synchronize.

"That's my girl," he said, and I lost it. Right there on the corner of high school and trashy novels, I fell into the chemical love of pre-teens whacked-out on romantic sugar. Such a small statement to capture a guarded woman like me, but it radiated that rare form of authentic endearment so lost in modern compliments and pick-up lines are a pet peeve of mine that has kept me single.

I was curious enough to wonder where this breezy male paragon actually *had* been all my life? He had an engaging telephone style and a sexy radio voice – that 'Robert Redford narrating a documentary on wolves' sort of voice.

We exchanged contact emails and fax numbers.

"My name is Jon without the 'h' Locke with an 'e'," he said. It was a quick, rehearsed spelling.

"I'm not usually an Alba. My friends call me Scottie. That's Scottie with an 'ie' instead of a y", I replied. "Watson with nothing of note to embellish it."

Woo Woo VERONICA KNOX

"Nonsense. If you say it a different way it's a hip question: what's on? I'm honored to be your friend after such a bizarre introduction. I look forward to hearing more about that monkey of yours."

"How long have I got?"

"If you can get everything to me yesterday, that would be great."

"Not a problem," I said.

All things considered – Jon's humor, his seductive charm, the killer voice, my imagination, the fact that I am a non-believer of anything paranormal, and adjusting for the cruel ironies of Mother Nature, I figured he probably looked like an Orc warrior on a bad day, but I decided to enjoy the fantasy while I could. I had never been 'someone's girl' quite that fast. It was a sweet illusion to keep me entertained while I searched my resources for trivia and dates anchored in the historical record. Anything for that voice and the chance of another off-chance endearment.

Jenner gazed up at me with canine pleading. "I know, I know," I said. "I'm nuts and you need to go."

I have discovered an oddity about research: relevant facts tend to rush to the scene of a request and, more curiously, these random acts of surprise are often the details which lead into the crux of a more intriguing subject. But I wasn't thinking this as I shuffled and scanned the local files: G for ghosts, T for tennis, H for hauntings, S for social clubs, and P for paranormal activity. That's when I cast my eyes on a headline that sucked me in, sure as a black hole on Star Trek. Up popped a photograph and an article under T with the headline: 'Tennis Club Mystery Man – is this Emily Carr's lost love?'

I am loathe to say it now, but sepia photographs of extinct families *haunt* me. I am captivated by old snapshots of my adopted city as it once was: dirt streets, horse-drawn carriages, grim penetrating eyes under black bowlers and the ridiculous mutton chops, beards, and formal frock coats of the serious businessman of an era long gone, and especially the women with enormous feathered hats and narrow waists.

I'm mesmerized by the solemn faces of children who had eventually grown into senility or were long-since struck down in infancy from deaths worse than fate. I meet their pets and playthings, and watch them play with incredibly static toys.

Photographic images of yesteryear are like books; I read each square through an invisible overlaid grid and translate. As an academic investigator it's my job and pleasure to pore over them with a professional state-of-the-art magnifying glass.

I reach into the snapshots of frozen brown and white life and listen. I'm no psychic nor a believer in the channeling claims of the spiritualist, but I am keenly empathic to distant sighs and laughter. I walk their streets as far as I can. I venture into their drawing rooms and garden parties. I mingle.

For the Victorian society ladies in the archives, it had been all tea and lace. Grunt work (barring childbirth, pardon the graphic reference) was passed to the servitude of foreigners.

I push my mind to experience summers with

WooWoo VERONICA KNOX

no ice or air-conditioning, and winters without thermostats or tumble dryers. I feel the soft jersey of my T-shirt turn into the scratch of starched linen. I imagine typing a letter on a noisy contraption that tries to eat your fingers and clacks away, fit to wake the dead.

Emily's lost love hooked me from the start. The photo was candid – an informal tennis party lounging together under the sun. But what was exceptionally intimate, was the mystery man leaning against Emily's legs. Her eyes in the photograph met mine and dared me to challenge her right to such blatant imprudence. She was in her well-practiced 'coy' stage, and her expression glowered, "bite me" quite clearly, and I heard her defensive, "so what, it's my business!"

"Wouldn't you like to know," her eyes teased. It wasn't hard to see that Emily was a headstrong young lady with a penchant for trouble, and I was sad for her, knowing from her published memoirs what was to come on this diary day which had gutted her happiness so irrevocably.

From her satisfied expression, I deduced Emily's 'devastating incident' had not yet taken place. I fantasized that this was the shot which had captured Emily's last prime moments of self-assurance. Her confidence being unaware of its approaching ruin in the form of the very man reclining into her skirts with such cavalier bearing.

A shutter clicked. People stirred and stretched. Conversations resumed as life unfroze. Perhaps Emily had feigned disinterest, yet all the while following her infatuation as 'he' strolled out of sight and she moved after him towards a life-altering encounter, declaring herself too soon and too far.

If that impertinent camera were to have reassembled the party once more, the man in question may well have been favouring another pretty face, with a flustered Emily looking on, unwilling to be captured on the other side of love.

It would have been an injured shadow who returned to Carr House and spilled her hurt onto a cruel white page.

In my empathic state I sat beside Emily's bedside and watched as she closed up like a flower in the dark.

In the months to come a new determined Emily would emerge to counter the temporary shrinking violet victim, forged from confusion and humiliation – the precursor to the brave, daring, young thing who ran to the wildwood to escape her own pride, and in so doing, ran smack into the love I felt sure she was meant to have.

The unknown can be so achingly full of promise. For the next twenty-four hours I felt like a teenager. I reverted to a dreamy girl, stuck nose-first into a shameless romance novel of remarkably synchronistic kismet. It was not surprising that Emily's mystery man easily morphed into an image of the ethereal Jon, defender of wolves. In my head, it was 1889 and I met him for tea at the Empress, though it hadn't yet been built. Details are for the rational, and official reports. Jon and I strolled the harbor under a white parasol and kissed behind the Hotel Grand, as yet an unpromising sector of mudflat real estate.

Woo Woo   VERONICA KNOX

The fax slid out with a mechanical whir and settled in the cradle for incoming documents; his name in print jumped off the page: Jon. Very Lindbergh, I thought. My mind searched for more examples: there was Anne (with an e) Shirley, of Green Gables who had claimed it sounded more grand. And it was true, I had a friend in art school, last name Browne, who played merry hell if the 'e' were dropped or maligned. I wrote the name Emily Carr with one 'r' – Emily Car – it looked ridiculous and sank on the page. The difference was extraordinary.

My birth name is Alba, the original Gaelic name for Scotland. It has a hard edge, like a mouth full of vowels. I prefer Scottie. As I stared at a blank piece of paper, I noticed it had become covered in ciphers from a phantom hand: Alba Locke, Scotty Locke, Mrs. Jon Locke, Scottie Locke, Mrs. Alba Watson-Locke – the way a daydreaming girl casts a spell over a beloved's last name. I crumpled it and tossed it at a wastepaper basket the size of a vase and missed. I needed to focus. And I needed to get a larger catchall for literary flotsam, there was a lot of it going around.

Daring fate to conjoin one's name to a handsome voice is a pastime for women with too much romance on their hands. For me, it was a case of not enough. I could see very clearly that Scotty with a 'y' failed to deliver the smell of tartan and heather. Jon was right about the single letter anomaly. Words are alphabet pictures. Sound-bites with meaning. Nibblings of nuance.

My Jon, I speculated, would have to be tall with fair hair - a tousled ash-blonde Beatle cut, casually pushed to the side, falling back like an English schoolboy's mop after a spritely game of cricket. I pictured a navy-blue blazer with an embroidered crest peeping from under the flowing black robes of an Oxford scholar. He would ride a bicycle with panache. I decided a long, maroon and gold striped Hogwart's scarf would drape loosely around his neck.

My hero's clean-shaven complexion would showcase a rugged tan with space left for rosy cheeks. His eyes? Definitely deep Aegean blue, twinkling under come-to-bed lids, framed in thick lashes. The rest followed easily: movie-star teeth, musk to die for, and a sensuous mouth. He was completely cheeky, utterly charming, and lanky as a pop star. I had described Anthony Andrews, circa 1980 *Brideshead Revisited*, Justin Haywood of the *Moody Blues*, and Robert Redford's *Sundance Kid*, how to set myself up for a fall.

I have always been skeptical about love at first sight. I held that opinion at 4:55 p.m. on an ordinary Friday in September, but by 5:01, I had become a firm believer in love at first *sound*.

For amusement, I took a few minutes to google images of Anthony and Robert, then listened to 'Nights in White Satin' on my headphones while I took Jenner for a lope around Beacon Hill Park. After that I hit the old microfiche trail.

Woo Woo VERONICA KNOX

Sometimes since,
I have wondered
if it was some small boy's spirit
that really did come to play with me
in the old garden...
I don't remember
ever seeing Drummie's face.
That was an unimportant detail.

~ Emily Carr ~
Hundreds and Thousands

I was struck less by his looks
than by the fact that he was carrying
a large teddy-bear.
'That' said the barber,
was Lord Sebastian Flyte,
a most amusing young gentleman.

~ Evelyn Waugh ~
Brideshead Revisited

Working the Graveyard Shift

I answered Jon's petition with zeal. I plunged into his assignment and stayed with it till morning. I felt embarrassed that I wanted to please him, but I had made *him* a priority as much as his request. The break from the tedium of several boring projects energized me. A dormant feminine gene had been activated. Jon deserved the juice I had claimed impossible to deliver at short notice, and I needed to expand my territory into deeper troves of data than the essentials of black and white evidence. I had always enlivened my sepia obsessions with real colors. I also realized that I needed to get out more. Mole work was making me pale of mind as much as complexion.

Research is like a tree growing in reverse. I begin at the leaves and follow the leads into the roots. The roots are a labyrinth; the end of the search lies under the ever-reticent hooves of the minotaur. Sometimes he's friendly.

It's slow game of chess. Checkmate is rare. Usually, the best I can do is reduce the pieces to a handful of stalemates. The last moves are often so obscure that even the original players had been unaware of the details and consequences.

People like to think of facts as being black and white, but in my experience that is rarely the case. Facts are ephemeral entities. Events move on quickly to replace or bury the older ones. Human memories are flawed, diaries tend to wax poetic, and letters are full of innuendo only meaningful to the original recipients. The veil of time is not the filmy gauze of poets but a heavy curtain, and each chess-piece is a different color on a solid black board. Little ivory lies are the darkest lies of all – deliberate twists of human data meant to mislead from the off.

Sir Walter Scott summed up the business of sorting human knots when he penned: *Oh what a tangled web we weave when first we practice to deceive.* It's human nature to varnish, edit, and embellish; lies and truths are simply normal confusions of unrecorded time.

The task Jon set me took less than a day, and we agreed to meet at the James Bay Tearoom.

"You can't miss me," he said. "I will be the one wearing a cape, and a shirt with a big S on the front."

"And S is for, what? supernatural?"

"Serendipity."

"Serenity dip," I anagrammed. "Sorry, I can't help it. It's a natural side-effect of *haunting* words. Sorry again."

"Then, S is for subsequent possibilities," he said.

WooWoo VERONICA KNOX

I was scanning for other 'S' words equally pregnant with possibilities when there he was, freezing my hand in mid-air as I returned my poised cup to its saucer. I almost snorted my Earl Grey.

I recovered with what I hoped was grace. "Sebastian," I said, and extended my hand. "You didn't bring Aloysius?" I continued, and patted the child seat left on one of the chairs. "And I ordered him a special seat."

Jon didn't miss a beat. "Lady Julia I presume?"

This tète a tète was either going to be fun or excruciatingly painful.

It was the school scarf that unnerved me more than anything else: pure Gryffindor. The ash blonde was more silver-fox, otherwise I had done a bang-up job of manifesting a fictional character, who carried off more youth at forty-one than any man had the right to. It was possible, at twenty-seven, that I was far too old for him.

Jon's ring finger was bare, and although it wasn't conclusive evidence of bachelorhood (considering I prided my research based on facts) my little heart sank: Jon was supermodel bait. Somewhere in this guy's background lurked a trophy girlfriend. Maybe two.

One thing for sure, Jon was not a floating bio-sample of lonely testosterone, waiting for... well, to put it bluntly, me. He was out of my league and my fantasy popped like a soap bubble on a hedgehog. The sounds of the cafe rushed into my ears and I heard my dreams snicker in the ether.

I felt the immediate smart from being pre-dumped in a life that lured with plastic carrots. I elected that fate had to be a woman. Mother

Nature's twin sister."She plays with us Sabu," I thought to myself, adapting one of my favorite lines from *Out of Africa*. No way was I giving Jon or her the benefit of the doubt; I was going to be cool.

The hour I thought must have passed had been a nanosecond of right-brain interference. I steadied myself and faced the silence as the orchestral swell of movie violins abruptly cut to real time.

The sounds of murmuring conversations filled the space between us. The background music was barely audible. The instrumental being played was 'It Had To Be You'. I remembered because when time stops and love hits you upside the head, one pays attention. Fate has an uncanny partnership with irony or was it sarcasm? One of my least favorite S words.

"Will you take tea?"I said, in keeping with my Oxford fantasy, and waved him into the empty chair.

"Tea and what?" he asked, pulling the chair closer.

"Tea and plovers eggs?" I suggested.

"How about tea and sympathy. My meeting got cancelled. The deal is unlikely. Dead in the water, to coin an apt phrase."

"Tea and chocolate then. I insist. And some ideas. No need for them to go to waste."

Jon produced a green I-Pad from his briefcase and flipped open its cover, ready to talk business. He opened a file, and his beautifully manicured fingers tap-danced over the screen – a magician conjuring bits of puzzle, dragging them into a coherent pattern. I watched, enraptured as a dog staring down a hamburger, kept my voice casual, and

WooWoo VERONICA KNOX

ordered a Triple Brownie Overload with raspberry reduction and whipped cream. I played easy-to-get and asked for two forks.

Jon was ready for my low-tech manila folder. "Too bad you no longer need this, it contains juice," I said.

"I'm still hoping for a juicy confession. Excuse me... interview," he said smiling. His eyes assessed me as he accepted my user-friendly data. Our hands touched with static electricity and burned me to the ground, but his voice was as steady as a Utah mountain top. "Tennis anyone?" he asked, with that damned Gatsby grin.

"Love 40 old sport," I thought, *"that's my boy."*

By anyone's reckoning, it had only been a matter of hours from our initial connection until we met to exchange information, and as it turned out, mutual lust.

I credit the divine afternoon of extra-sensory perfection to the cocoa bean wizards of Switzerland. As I had long-suspected, fate *was* a woman, and I sent her a hasty, chocolate-covered apology by re-dubbing her, My Fair Lady, the fairest of them all.

S is for sparks.

THE SISTERS
GRIMM

Once upon a time,
a princess named Emily,
was visited by a knight
who wished to make her his lady.
The knight declared his love
and asked for her hand,
but it was long before the days when Emily realized
she was imprisoned in a tower called society,
and that she may actually like to be rescued.
Like most youngest daughters in a fairy tale,
Emily had a pair of harridans for sisters,
who were jealous of her charms.
They treated her cruelly and lied to her about love.
Emily refused her prince and the dragons came,
and the walls of her castle grew cold.
Eventually, the heartbroken knight married another.
And even though Emily saved herself in the end,
she had saved herself too literally at the expense of love.
Guilt grew thorns around Emily's soul
and a hundred years passed.
Timing is everything,
and it can change
on a dime.

~ Scottie Watson ~

Somebody else was there too.
He was on a white horse
and he had brought another white horse
for me.

~ Emily Carr ~
The Book of Small

Once Upon a Dime

I never considered having a dog, two cats, and a limitless selection of books for companions, as settling for less. My calendar was not a flat grid of blank lily pads. On the contrary, I was busy enough to cherish the free time I did have. Bringing one's work home is unavoidable when your office is in the corner of your living room. I made a concerted effort to separate myself from the ongoing piles of projects which made shuffling noises from time to time while I was enjoying a recreational book.

Jenner's bodily needs keep me tuned to the streets. He is the surrogate dad to the pair of cats who followed us home from the local animal shelter. He's allowed one bark when we can see our front door – the equivalent of 'Honey, I'm home' that he sends from the epicentre of the old orchard of St. Ann's on Humboldt Street. From there I can see the answering 'what did you bring me?' of two blobs of fur, pacing the wide windowsills of my second floor suite.

Dolly is a feline version of an Alaskan husky – she

has a coat of white and grey patches, with a tail that curls over her back in the continuing defense from the human cruelty she suffered before she came to me. Her best buddy is an abandoned golden ex-tom named Lucozade, whose size makes Garfield look like an orange mouse. Technically, they both belong to Jenner.

I am allowed to provide food, and share 85 % of my bed with them from midnight to alarm clock. The four of us have formed a mutual admiration society worth it's weight in sanctuary. A man is a fleeting daydream who intrudes from time-to-time. A sweet-scented phantom man, who puts the toilet lid down and leaves before dawn.

After meeting Jon, my logic did a *one-eighty*. Life turns on a coin-toss – a thin dime of fate. Academic research is a solitary job. It used to be enough.

"Is it a prince you wait for?"
"I wait for no one. I came to London to study."

~ Emily Carr ~
Growing Pains

The Voice of Reason

o, when I started to hear Emily speaking to me at odd times of the day, I didn't pay much attention until I saw her standing at the foot of my bed, scowling. She was not happy. I was not happy. She was a terrifying apparition.

Emily first appeared to me the night after I visited The Ross Bay Cemetery and eaten take-out curry from a dodgy restaurant, and so I put the experience down to indigestion and an overactive imagination. I had gone to bed with a handful of antacids, thinking of her, having pulled out the copy of her complete literary works to read while the peppermint medicine took effect – the very book that had set me back fifty dollars when I was extremely low on funds. I had purchased it after being in Victoria for a few days, as I wanted to know everything about the curious Miss Carr. That was twelve months ago, at the tail end of a move to escape the winters of Alberta.

2012 is a significant year as it turned out. Emily was clear about this. She was clear about a lot of things. Especially, that she had no intention of leaving me anytime soon. Her tenacious reputation precedes her, but I too, am known for being stubborn at the core. Another reason to suspect we might be related, but no, just in time, I regained my senses. I may be on a paranormal detour, but I still don't believe in heaven, hell, Shangri-La or reincarnation. I don't believe in ghosts either, but it turns out they scare me sideways, anyway. Especially one with an expression that can curdle cream.

Emily decided to stay auditory for now. Sometimes she is muddled – a tad lost, but usually she is adamant (read aggressive) about her intentions. She has a task for me, but she has to connect and win my cooperation first. She has to test me. I had survived the ghastly first hurdle – the visitation. Next will come promptings, and I am directed to do some research.

"Pretend to write a book about me," she ordered. "Dig around."

"Or what?" I asked defiantly.

Her heavy chuckle came as a companionable wheeze. I had passed test two.

Perhaps it was the combination of my proximity to Emily's physical remains, trailing around her homestead, and retracing the steps from her home-to-home hopscotch years in James Bay that had something to do with it. I was intrigued. Emily Carr hadn't really been much of a mystery during her life of seventy-four years, but like all legends, she *had* become one.

Emily loomed large in every way; she was hardly a covert character. Her views were written in

WooWoo VERONICA KNOX

up-front language and boomed heartily, startling conversations with undisguised bravado. Random shyness sideswiped her occasionally, but she always recovered. She became the quintessential plain-spoken, 'tough old bird'.

The only time Emily held back was disclosing her love-life. Now it seemed she was ready to redress the secrecy. Honesty had gotten the better part of pride. It was time, she said, to 'spill her beans' and did I want to know more?

"Saying and telling are different," Emily informed me. "This is going to be a telling. One needs a good telling off every so often," she said, and I wasn't sure if she was referring to herself or me.

"Seeing is believing," I retorted. "Can you show yourself again as well as tell?"

She was blunt. "In good time," she said, which meant in 'Emily time'.

"Listening and hearing are different as well," I said. Which do you prefer?"

Her voice paused to examine me for flaws. It seemed an age before she answered. "We will have a no-nonsense hearing followed by a great deal of doing. If you say yes."

"And if I don't?"

"You have to."

"Why? How?... Who says?"

"You're indebted to me."

"Scuze me?"

"I gave you the colors and the light. Remember?"

I searched the past she was quoting, and caught my admiration and gratitude after seeing her paintings for the first time. She was right.

"Never make passionate declarations lightly,"

she admonished. "Especially ones about art. Creativity isn't just an empty word."

"I've learned that about words lately," I said. "So, I created an obligation then?"

"You forged a bond, my dear."

"Oh, happy day."

"It could be if you play my cards right," she said.

Emily was a woman with complications of family Carr dysfunction. As an artist, she had a wee blighty of personal chemical imbalance. The positive kind, that walks the thin edge of creative entitlement. She had been confused and encouraged as a girl – given the freedom to roam in the garden clear through to Beacon Hill Park, yet confined to a narrow road of stringent discipline. Ironically, she became a bully to counteract being bullied.

Had I been honoured or cursed? It was hard to tell, but most often, it was the former. I'd checked out Emily's childhood haunts and now I was over my head in an advanced metaphysics class.

We arranged that our next conversation would take place after a silent walk together in Beacon Hill Park. I had an inkling that she would join me as an apparition and startle the bejeezus out of me, so having Jenner along felt reassuring.

I assumed Emily was with me as I climbed the hill. Somehow, I had the idea that animals were attuned to ghosts and I felt safe. Emily loved dogs, so I figured she would manifest the sweeter side of her curmudgeon persona.

I am so naive, but at least I may soon be 'bejeezus-free', for what that's worth.

I poured Jenner a bowl of water and stared at the ocean and the majestic mountain peaks across the strait that looked like icebergs floating in the sky. I refused to ask the standard opening question: 'Are you there?' Instead, I got down to business and spoke aloud. "We have to have some ground rules" I announced, addressing the trees and squirrels as much as anything or anyone. It was not a suggestion. Jenner twitched his ears.

"We both need to," came the reply from a respectful distance away.

Jenner remained nonplussed. He had dropped to a restful repose after his long lope along the beach and a steep midday climb. He had fallen asleep or Emily had cast a spell on him.

"Absolutely no more midnight visitations, for a start," I said, peering towards the disembodied voice. "My nerves won't take it and I need my sleep."

"My nerves understand your nerves," she said. "I was none too stable myself at your age."

"And now?"

"Being dead is as stable as it gets," she said.

We would wing the rest of the rules. For now, Emily had chosen to manifest as the disembodied voice I first encountered in the cemetery. Thoughts that she may suddenly materialize did nothing to ease my nerves, but I managed to laugh about the various states of molecular instability with her before Jenner and I headed for home.

I became aware that the simple weight of an apartment key in my pocket felt good. A small sign of physical life – a simple thing taken for granted. I was real. The key proved it.

The rooms behind my front door welcomed me with a personal invitation. I felt pumped; my decor appeared more in focus. My eclectic furnishings invited me to sit and absorb their forms and colors. I kept the lights dimmed, lit a few candles and some sticks of sandalwood incense, and wandered to the window where I stood gazing dreamily into the grounds of St. Ann's Academy below.

Not much had changed since Emily's time. The Autumn leaves were brittle and ready to fall. Already a gold carpet was weaving over the lawns. A pungent promise of pumpkin spice hung in the air that blew through the mosquito-screened window. It had been a dry summer, too hot for my definition of comfort, and I was ready for the rains of October. Humboldt Street was quiet except for the clip-clop of a horse-drawn tourist carriage. I saw the driver pause her horse so her passengers could better view the display of mellowing trees. It might have been 1912.

I spared a thought for all the lost lovers who tried to turn for home and were too late. The ones who bravely moved on in spite of the lonely anguish knowing they'd botched their one chance for optimum happiness.

The human body is capable of and culpable for emotional mistakes, but what if the love of one's life shows up after one is dead? Maybe, sometimes, it takes death to fall in love.

I can't marry you, Martyn.
It would be wicked and cruel,
because I don't love that way.

~ Emily Carr ~
Growing Pains

Who Knew? ... Woo Knew

o began my friendship with Emily Carr. Her teenage heart-attack (at seventeen) was her name for the denied love that stung and crushed her deeply. Trusting and trysting came hard after that. She asked permission to materialize, and as it was broad daylight, I was less afraid.

The definitive Emily appeared, natural as the trees and grass, a cuddly old-dear dressed in shapeless black. I say shapeless, but she was a pyramid mound. A human hill with a kind smile.

I was disappointed at first. "Where's Woo? I asked.

"I'm not Long John Silver," she retorted in a huff, but she understood. The eccentric image of a Victorian crone 'a la Saint Francis' with a monkey on her shoulder was to be expected and even cherished. She was a woman not an archetype, and not about to promote her iconic cachet, but I hoped it may arrive later in the form of her pet, Woo.

"Why did you wear a hairnet all the time?" I asked her, cheekily.

"It's not" she snapped, smile gone. "It's a headband. It defines me. Confines my thoughts. It comforts me, stops headaches, and grounds me. Is that enough reason?"

"More than enough. If it does all that, I should get one for myself," I said.

Searching for a new topic, I asked Emily how she could bear hanging around that bleak spot, called her resting place.

"I'm not sleeping there in a box," she said, all the while looking at me as if I were an imbecile. "What do you imagine?" she went on, "an underground city of the dead? A rabbit warren of ghoulish garden parties?"

In my defense, I stood my ground. "It is certainly one of the darkest gardens I have yet to visit," I replied. "I hope you're partying in heaven then."

Emily harrumphed loudly. "Woman, you must calm yourself. You're speaking in fairytales. Leave your little girl notions behind. We have grown up problems to forge."

I asked her if I could share our rendezvous with Jon and she made me promise not to until she gave the all-clear. Reluctantly, I obeyed, too intimidated to quibble.

We spent a good hour establishing how, where, and when we would meet. I wanted to know if others could see her. She said only the ones who were daydreaming, but she relieved my mind of one thing: we would be mental conversationalists. I would not be seen muttering to myself whenever we needed to converse. Generally, people were too absorbed in getting somewhere or texting on their cell phones to notice a women talking to herself, but I didn't want to chance it. I reckoned I could always

WooWoo VERONICA KNOX

hold my mute phone to my ear and speak into it any time Emily and I spoke in public.

With Emily it was touch and go. She had the double-touch of Medusa and Midas about her. Emily's looks could kill, but her words offered a golden opportunity that promised lucrative resources of tangible treasure. However, as all fairy-tale treasures, there was a catch with disproportionate negative consequences.

Emily's flack was an automatic defense from her own insecurity. My words could injure her as much as hers could unnerve me, and I understood, that although I could break the ice with sarcasm, it inevitably left a verbal ice pick in Emily's hands and she knew how to wield it.

Emily loved to keep me on my toes. The next time we met in the park, she was a young woman, the same age as me, and her riding costume dazzled me. Rosy high cheekbones, seductive eyes and all, were a pleasant shock. I must have looked surprised.

"I wasn't always the default crone," she said.

"No, of course not," I said. "You look unbelievably uncomfortable in that corset and tightly-laced boots."

"I was, but I don't have to suffer that now. Fashion was always a damned nuisance," she winked. "I feel as ethereal as a vapour. Weightless. And once I decided to stay unmarried, the corset came off," she laughed. "And I never looked back. Long-live the artist's smock! I was free – physically and emotionally."

"But not sexually," I said, without thinking.

There was an uncomfortable pause where I was burned through with a pair of hurt grey eyes. Emily returned to her definitive old lady garb.

"No. Not that. Bring a notebook the next time, and by the way, you might pay more attention to details. That chattering you heard in the cemetery? It was a monkey."

If you go down in the woods today
you're sure of a big surprise
If you go down in the woods today
you'd better go in disguise.

~ lyrics to *'Teddy Bear's Picnic'*
James Kennedy
1934

Today's the Day

I thought Jon had been humoring me when he took me antiquing on one of our first official dates, but he was into old items with 'Velveteen Rabbit' psychometric ambiance. Our weekend outings, trolling for curios were a source of mutual pleasure.

Once, we came across a wicker doll's pram in a shop window, displaying a teddy-bear that had been through several generations of childhood wars. A white cotton bandage had been wrapped around its ear by the owner of the shop. It was early 1870's, not for sale, but Jon took a picture of me holding it, hoping for an image of one of it's owners hovering nearby.

Early October was still beach weather, so Jon and I usually found a quiet spot near the water, sitting on driftwood logs, to enjoy a relaxed picnic. It was still too hot to be car-friendly weather for dogs, though the rainy season was fast approaching, so restaurant lunches were still reduced to overcast days or sidewalk cafes.

We had opened a thermos of tea and unwrapped our sandwiches, when I noticed a gaggle of dogs down the beach. The woman herding them looked like Emily, and my conversation faltered, leaving an unfinished sentence hanging in a speech bubble.

Jon followed my gaze and found nothing of obvious interest. "You okay?" he asked, and I gave him a reassuring smile.

"Sorry, what was I saying? I lost my chain ... er... of..." I started, but my words trailed into a salty wisp of imagination. It *was* Emily. I knew it was her because she waved to me and called, "Hellooooo Scottie." In her hand was a narrow band of black cloth and her hair flew about her face like a halo. Her 'hairnet'.

"I had thought you hung on my every word," Jon teased. "You wandered off somewhere. Or did you see something?"

"Just a dog," I said. "It's gone. I was checking to see if it was a Jenner challenge."

The breeze of Emily and her entourage brushed past my arm in a rush of snuffles and growls. I saw Jenner's ears twitch towards them, but he had been staring out to sea and was now focused on some newly-landed gulls hopping near us for scraps.

I heard Emily's voice say: "Nice day," and move off into the surf. Her presence disturbed the seagulls and sent them away in a scare of curses, and Jenner rested his shaggy head on his paws again.

Blue-sky peace settled on our family of three, and I made a silent note to come clean to the lovely, trusting man across from me, who raised his ham

WooWoo VERONICA KNOX

sandwich to the waves and toasted me in yet another admission of my perfection.

Jon loved ghosts and ghostly conversations and ghostly problems, so my ghostly secret haunted me as much as Emily taunted me. It was exasperating to have made a promise to a sea-witch with a macabre sense of humor. I was still being tested.

Following Emily's promising breadcrumbs was not without danger. They could lead me to a witchy oven, hotter than her temper, door open wide... the whole loaf inside baited with a butter and jam. She wanted me to tag along, and by *tag* she meant understand. Her thoughts have evolved since her death (so she declared), much has been revealed and she is keen to find her lost man.

Woo's ashes, tossed into the winds of Stanley Park have long-since blown over the Strait of Georgia, and settled on her mistress's grave to be lovingly absorbed, dust-to-dust.

I finally met Miss Woo. I had been daydreaming – staring off into the trees, and noticed a red dot bouncing from leaf-to-leaf like the 'follow the dancing ball' graphics on a karaoke screen. "She was never that colour," I declared.

"Woo is a chameleon," Emily said proudly. "She's rarely the same shade twice, but she favours red and her default fur is no colour at all. She seems made of clear glass in her natural state. Naturally she was brown for the duration of her lifetime."

As Woo came closer she changed colour several times.

"She's showing off," Emily said.

When she reached Emily, Woo was the colour and consistency of a shaft of moonlight. A moonbeam that chirped a song of innocent welcome.

Monkey business has hit the fan. My fan. Now I hear the scratching of monkey fingers at the door, and once, my perfectly stable phone ejected its own receiver from its cradle. I found it on the floor, where I most certainly did not place it. Mercifully, it jumped to freedom when I wasn't around.

Memories of the *Monkey's Paw* story filtered back to me and made me sweat at night. Scratch that... perspire with awareness. There goes that language trap again.

Jenner sniffed cautiously into the corners of our apartment and made high-pitched whines in the back of his throat. I woke once, with him sleeping on top of me, which was quite the experience. Irish wolfhounds have lapdog desires that coincide with nature's sense of humor.

In the meantime, nightmares became the anticipated visions which might appear between consciousness and sleep. Those last limbo seconds when one's guard is down and the doors of the dreamtime are thrown open to the whims of spontaneous visitation.

"Why Emily," I protested. "Why on middle earth, would you burn the very love letters you kept as treasures? Kept, I might add, when they might, I say *might* have been socially-controversial in a *good* way?"

"I was in a foul temper," she shot back. "Clearing out the old house, and the spring cleaning bug bit

WooWoo VERONICA KNOX

me. I wanted to burn half my paintings too. I wanted to burn my guilt most of all. I was angry. Looking back on my mistakes made me livid. There's no fool like an old, untidy, sentimental fool!"

"Or an angry one."

"I was making a statement."

"By murdering love?"

"By staying mum. By staying *me*. I didn't like all the poking. I had some fame coming, I could smell that. It was too late, and snoops get into your privacy like mice. Martyn was still living. They would have found him and I couldn't bear that. His annual Christmas 'flower letter' had arrived, and in a pique I sacrificed it on my New Year's Eve hearth. It was symbolic."

"Of what? Some poetic resolution?"

Emily's defensive blustering retreated to remorse. "It was pathetic. I didn't deserve such kindness. I never returned the favour even though there was a return address. He must have hoped."

I watched Emily dream herself into a stupor of memories before I spoke again, trying to be sprightly, "perhaps not writing was the kindest thing."

"Martyn had the kindness I reserved for animals. There's no point in whitewashing. I was not being cruel-to-be kind. I 'bucketed' Martyn's love from fear. To save myself."

I shuddered. I had read of Emily's matter-of-fact method of dispatching her ailing puppies by drowning. It even made me hate her a little. She had the strength I hoped I would never have to display. Emily's Victoria of the frontier was a harsher time. I suspect I would have made a crappy pioneer, but a way tougher landlady.

My van elephant
is now a reality.
While she sat there in the lot
she was only a dream shaping itself.
She was bought so suddenly
after long years of waiting.
It is two months from the morning
that I got out of bed at 5 a.m.
to peep out of the studio window
and see if she was really there in the lot beneath.
Then came all the fixings,
meat safe, dog boxes and monkey-proof corner.
And when she was ready,
equipped in full,
the hauler came and said that it was impossible
to get her out of the lot
because she was too low,
and he was horrid and I was mad.
"Well" I said,
"if the man brought her 3,370 miles
across the Rockies,
surely she can be taken twelve miles
to Goldstream Flats.

~ Emily Carr ~
Hundreds and Thousands

There (the elephant) sat,
her square ugliness
bathed in the summer sunshine,
and I sang in my heart.

~ Emily Carr ~
Hundreds and Thousands

The Elephants in the Room

"That hindsight thing being 20/20 is true," I said to Emily. She nodded slowly. "I know something now that I never guessed in life. Woo used to move a small ivory elephant about the house," she said, "I found it in the oddest places. The drawer of my night table, the fridge, beside the phone, inside my handbag or a shoe.

You see, I ignored the phone when I was painting. Occasionally, Woo reacted to a call by dancing around it agitated to beat all. It was one of those candlestick affairs, easy to knock over. If she fussed I would have to stop and replace the receiver, thrown to the floor. I hadn't understood. I think Jane, my cockatoo, tried to translate a few times.

"She screened your calls. Handy little wench," I said.

I picked up the ornament at a church jumble sale and nicknamed it Jumbo for fun, you know, after the famous elephant from the London Zoo, but when my sister Alice misheard me and remarked disdainfully, that it was 'pure jumble all right', I renamed it. Woo liked to use Jumble as a paperweight, but only letters from Martyn warranted its protection.

I always returned the little ivory beast to its regular spot on the mantel. I first thought that I had a poltergeist, but it was the minx. Now I know it was her way of communicating that something important needed my attention."

Blending into the wild forests of Sooke isn't easy for a large grey cube named 'the elephant'. Emily's caravan of delights was heavy and cumbersome: her twin. Her doppelganger pal who shared her scorn for civilization or the need for dainty accommodation. Roughing-it was the law according to Carr. Emily's Law.

Old photographs show Emily sitting hunched around her campfire as Klee Wyck, the laughing one, claiming her centre of gravity. The wild-woman who knows all – 'The Delphi of Goldstream', pushing green logs onto the fire, calling down the moon, chanting for rain to keep out trespassers.

The 'Elephant' was a large grey studio – a portable zoo, and Emily's confession booth. It sheltered her from emotional and elemental weather by removing its occupants to higher ground. If Emily was Mother Noah, this elephant was surely her ark.

Campsite photos from 1933 show a 'nativity scene' of animals arranged around a central figure. One or two visiting 'dignitaries' hover in the background, all posed around the goddess of prickly pear philosophy, and her monkey.

I studied the faces and the vanishing point, and discovered something: Emily, her entourage, and the camera were all focused on Woo.

It was Woo, not Emily, who was the epicenter of the grotto. It was, in effect, Woo's elephant, Woo's theatre, and Woo's travelling show. She was 'Queen of the Hill'.

Like me with my own menagerie, Emily was allowed to serve.

I took my leave of Emily and left her in the park, soon after her ivory elephant story. I had a dinner date with Jon and what turned out to be a third 'elephant in the room'.

Our dessert came with a chocolate sauce. Ever the gallant, Jon let me have the first bite and waited till it was savoured and reviewed. I gave it three stars out of five, but instead of taking a taste, Jon picked up my hand and kissed it. His eyes were dialled to romantic smolder for effect. The moment was set for some serious delivery.

I waited, nervously. Finally, he spoke in a mock business-like voice: "It's time for the monkey ghost," he insisted.

"You don't think you're being a tad quixotic?" I said, taking back my hand.

"Whimsy is underestimated," he replied.

"I'm going to need a fresh pot of tea, then."

For my amusement, Jon clicked his fingers together to summon an invisible waiter.

"Garcon, mademoiselle requires one of your finest pots of ze Early Grey, immédiatement."

"Funny, I don't see him," I said. "Is he a ghost?"

"Au contraire ma petite. He is an enchanted chimpanzee."

"*My* monkey was a girl."

Jon gave me a surprised look, "well, that's a good place to start," he said.

I told Jon about Marmie, my pocket-size plush monkey toy with no tail (a design oversight by Steiff, its manufacturer). I explained how Marmie was my confessor and that I told her everything and plagued her with questions. She was privy to all because I took her everywhere with me.

"Marmie had a shadow," I said, "metaphorically speaking, she cast a larger shadow, but the one I'm talking about moved. This one had a tail."

Jon poured the tea and pushed the cup towards me. He was like a kid hearing a fairytale.

I called my toy Marmie, after Marmee, the mother in *Little Women*, long before I learned that the species of monkey that visited me was a marmoset. I never thought of it as a ghost and I called her Marmie 2. So, there's another 'ie' versus a double 'ee' spelling to add to your list," I said.

Marmie's arms were designed to hold a bendy pose so she could cling to places and hold things. Every Easter Sunday, my mother set Marmie on my dresser and gave her a miniature cream egg to hold.

Marmie was forever wandering off. I found her all over the house and sometimes in the garden where I was certain I hadn't left her.

I tested Marmie's magic with harmless wishes. I would touch an object I didn't mind losing and walk to the end of our garden path. Then I wished it to disappear and returned to the scene of the innocent crime. It was always gone. I had a doll's pram that finally collapsed from missing bolts and screws. I was punished for not taking care of it. I protected Marmie and confessed to my mother it was my secret power, as I had made the wishes.

My punishment had been for telling fibs as much as destroying an expensive toy. My father and I repaired the pram together. Finally I polished it and filled it with my best linen doll bedding. I hadn't known the last step: he donated it to the poor.

"Dad wheeled it away and left me sobbing into Marmie as if she were a handkerchief. When I looked up the pram was gone, and from the corner of my eye, I saw Marmie 2. She was, literally, hopping mad. She leapt to the curtains and swung there. Then, she dropped onto my bed, looked into my eyes with deep compassion, and melted away like the Cheshire Cat in *Alice in Wonderland*.

After that, whenever Marmie 2 paid Marmie and I a visit, I asked for Marmie 2-sized wishes."

"Do you remember any of them," Jon asked.

"I wished I could grow up with no-one to boss me around. Little Marmie disappeared the time we moved, when I was ten.

"I was ten when I saw my ghost too," Jon said.

"Did yours have a name?"

"She was a four-year-old girl. The classic invisible playmate, but more. She told me her name was Click and that she had died."

"I was four when I got Marmie."

"There's a hidden 'key' and the word 'money' inside the word monkey," Jon said, hastily adding "No, I'm serious" when he saw me smile. "It's the whole, six degrees of etymology thing," he insisted. "No word is an island."

My brain warmed to Jon's theory and recognized a hit: "the original meaning for the word occult was 'hidden'," I said. "It's only time and misuse that have rendered it dark and sinister."

Jon grinned his admiration, "my point exactly."

WooWoo

Dear Martyn,
because he loved me, he went away.

~ Emily Carr ~
Growing Pains

Valentine Massacre

Emily was being facetious about her first heart attack. She meant a broken heart, of course. Her chemicals had been spurned. It was pure, simple, and extremely powerful: a cosmic biology lesson. One never forgets the first rejection. "The vividness of it is preserved in amber," she said, and added, "it was more uncomfortable than a honeyed tomb... it was more like being pickled in vinegar. It stung."

I waited for more, but she shrugged and shuffled into silence before brightening, "I have *you* to change it! You will un-pickle my stupidity and fear."

Emily took my silence for agreement. The enormity of her faith in me left me momentarily speechless. Finally, I erupted in my own declaration of limitations:

"What makes you so sure a mortal such as myself, can do such a thing? What is it in your twisted mind that assumes I can or will attempt such a bizarre mission?"

Emily examined her fingernails. "Are you going to psychoanalyse me?" she asked, casually.

"Well, I can, but it's rather debatable isn't it?"

"Speak plainly."

"Pointless."

Dear 'Millie' was not exactly cut from heart-to-heart cloth. I invited her to a proper English picnic tea with plum cake, and china cups and saucers, hoping for a 'lady's fingers and sherry' conversation. Some kind of girlfriend talk. "Did you kiss Martyn?" I asked in my best high-school pant.

She raised her eyebrows. "As if *that* was the most memorable thing about me or us," she said.

Madame Woo snatched my cup and turned it upside down. She took one look inside the emptied cup and ran off, demented as a tealeaf reader with a terrible prophecy.

"So it *was* William, a.k.a Martyn, then," I said, triumphantly.

"I called him Will or Billy. Martyn was his pseudonym."

"A love by any other name," I quoted.

"People seem to like that you were real enough to spurn and be jilted," I remarked. "It makes you less of a curmudgeon – a reputation I might add, that you did nothing to check."

"Like everyone, I had a few secrets."

"Secrets sell more books," I said. "A volume of your love letters fanned by the press from diary to shoebox would have been been a bestseller, but you had to do the predictable Victorian thing and burn them. Were they that risqué?"

"Not at all. My personal diaries were ..."

"Edited?"

"Selective."

"You mean safe," I ventured.

"I mean, none of your business," she said.

"I want to listen to you, it's just that I can't take more of your endless 'Green Woman' botany lessons, okay? I have read them all. Woodland flora and fauna adventures are for the keen of camping. Which, I am absolutely, not. I happen to be seriously camping-phobic. So, enough. I get it. Effusing over pinecones and ozone is overkill."

Emily looked miffed, "I see you won't stop till I play you a big love story."

"Besides, don't your paintings say it all? Isn't a picture of nature supposed to be worth a thousand words?"

"I will give you a few about Will (Martyn to you) and you're not to pester me further, mind."

"Background with juice please," I begged. "I shall use my extraordinary *will*power to desist."

Emily shook out her long skirts and made herself more comfortable. The freshness of youth infused her hourglass form with grace. She was radiant. "I will paint you a brief history," she said. "William and I met on board the *Willapa*. There was something brewing in the sea; something surrounding us in a bubble that gave him courage and me a heightened sense of curiosity. Then, as we inched close enough to breach the code of courtly conduct, a gull screeched and the spell burst like fireworks, but we were both left intrigued."

"I know the feeling."

"We were moved, altered forever."

"I'm not hearing details," I reminded.

"I closed, Scottie. Snap! – like a scary book. The

more I stepped back, Will advanced closer to peer behind my speeches of protest. I needed time; he expected a rushing in of souls. Well, mine rushed all right, it ran for cover."

"Tell!"

Emily drew herself up and scanned me, pausing like a good storyteller before she spoke: "I felt every muscle tense up. My lips parted waiting for the bliss. I was about to faint and there was a disturbance. I felt it out the corner of my eye and the moment fizzled into an awkward silence. We shook hands and retreated to explore our lust in private. Smitten, okay?"

"Got it."

"Well, I felt too much. I needed air, and the wilderness I was headed to promised to stave off intruders, but William was not intruding; he was simply courting too fast. He wanted to consume me. He cramped my adventure. I was playing the selfless suffragette, chaining myself to a totem pole for the cause of the broken-hearted. Well, *my* cause. I was the maligned princess running with the deer for forest sanctuary. Martyn couldn't keep up or read the signs, so I left Canada."

Victoria's rules had overruled Martyn. I must have looked sad, but Emily exploded in anger, as if she needed to justify her actions.

"It was too soon for me to fall. Love faltered. I blamed the timing, but it was my red shoes twitching to be away, and I had the 'pioneer me' to follow. I saw myself running ahead, clearing the path, while the slower me followed the hem of my disappearing skirts and the broken branches that my cold determined self had left to guide that other me."

WooWoo VERONICA KNOX

"I see," I managed. Hardly a full response, but I had shared Emily's emotions as she re-lived the painful moment, and I was exhausted.

Emily had gone for survival over something she likened to male cannibalism. She mistook every hint of carnal love as a malicious sending to entrap vulnerable women.

Emily heard my thoughts and answered. "I believed that if I had surrendered, the artist me would have died, and some domestic shade would have possessed the space that was me. A negative space between the solid trees and rocks. As a girl, I was deeply invested in the fairy tale of Cinderella, but I grew up to fear glass slippers and their agendas of slavery. I wanted no midnight trysts above or below decks. I fancied myself a heroine. Oh, bosh and nonsense! Death is as unfair as life."

"I've yet to meet Klee Wyck," I said. "You must have projected a jovial personality to warrant the name 'laughing one'."

"People see what they see. Names stick with little provocation. I was in First Nation's territory. Out of my element. It behooved me to act friendly. Besides it masked the fear I sometimes felt. I was given the name Klee Wyck from people with little to laugh about, and yet they were refreshing next to my stuffy family. They fascinated me. I shed all my inhibitions of society and the suppressed wild-child in me returned. I was free. Laughter came easily as a young child. Klee Wyck was a time more than it was a name."

"So, you're the quintessential restless spirit?" I asked.

"I'm a puzzle."

"We have a three-dimensional puzzle called a Rubik's cube," I said, and I made the size and shape of it with my hands. "It has a different colour grid of squares on each side and an ingenious mechanism which one twists until the patterns are hopelessly confused. The game is returning the mixed up colours to their original state. You Miss Carr, are a steel Rubik's cube with attitude. You, Miss Emily, have sharp corners. You're not just a puzzle; you're an enigma. You are a sphinx."

I showed Emily the cube in my mind.

"I can see it just fine," she said.

She scrambled it for a while, before declaring it the perfect manifestation of love: twisted and always four moves from consummation. The deliberate angles of playing coy and the futile backtracking to that primal 'cube moment' when the pristine landscape had been simple planes of colour, before the loving.

"I am the stubborn yellow square lost in territorial green. It was a perfect metaphor for Martyn, the green square 'waiting on the other side', including the reference to death.

"Before you met Martyn, when you said you flirted so outrageously, were you just playing cat and mouse?" I asked.

"There's no 'just' about it. We called it being demure."

"We call that being a tease," I said, "well, that's the nicest thing we call it. In your day, a kiss must have been forward. Rather too daring."

"I was shocked to discover that I was the mouse for once. It shook me I can tell you."

"The tennis party man when you were seventeen?"

"I misread his interest as advances."

"Hardly misread. He kissed you, didn't he?"

"No. Pride made me write that. It was me. I kissed *him*."

"And?"

"And then I traipsed after him like a puppy and made a damned fool of myself."

"What did he do?"

"He took me down a peg, that's what! Me. Princess Emily. It was the first time that I experienced the male version of myself. He was a charming flirt, but it was a facade. They say 'pride goeth before a fall', but mine failed me, afterwards. I became wary of men, unable to trust my feelings. I think I was in shock. The whole incident cast a cloud over Victoria and my life, and I wanted to escape to a place where no-one knew me.

"So, art school in San Francisco?"

"So, San Francisco," Emily glowered.

"Emily, you were only following your instincts. It wasn't your fault that self-confidence was considered a sin. You were brave enough to risk everything. That couldn't have been easy."

"Bravery had nothing to do with it. It was pride. I was acting cheeky, as usual, from self-interest. Lizzie was there being a prude and I was showing off on purpose. More brazen and pushy than usual to show her up. Father had died and she was lording her smug values over me. But she won, I punished myself the rest of my life."

"And Martyn."

"Yes. Him most of all."

"You must have been quite the hussy," I ventured.

"I was the *coquette* – overconfidence made me conceited. Well, I had spurned my share of admirers before that day when that 'other one' devastated me. I have blocked his name from my memory. I dared love to happen often enough, and ten years later when it did, I ran to art again, with an excuse I could believe in."

"Were the terrors of love so indecent?" I asked.

"Feeling the shame of rejection was worse. It was a defining moment. I vowed to never feel that again. Since that moment, I was afraid of losing face. Holding back hurt less."

"Guilt conquers all," I said, "poor Martyn. Lousy timing."

"Martyn was compelling, but his eyes were frantic; he offered me fierce love. His eagerness demanded a choice. I gave him reason to hope when we became friends. We both drifted into different romantic fantasies. I fought with mine; he embraced his. While he stewed, I offered friendly courtship, safely protected from an actual conquest. It felt delightfully safe.

Much later, after London, when I saw Martyn in San Francisco, he was married and had made a hash of it, and I felt rescued by *her*, his *'surrogate'* wife. I had, by then, decided to be a spinster, so I could afford to feel jealous and slighted. That night I cried till sunrise and my headaches returned. I believed I had been delivered from a terrible fate, yet at the same time, I had evaded a great love. I have never been so angry with myself, or felt so wretched.

In our early courtship, Martyn became a regular addition at the Carr dining table. His conversations were carefully crafted to capture Lizzie and Alice. He thought that was a net for me too. Ha! It was the opposite. My sisters and I were always at odds, romancing them distanced me.

Martyn was so earnest and I was enchanted, but in denial – the put-upon princess, horrified while the frog-prince became more adamant. Games. How I played them to delay the world, thinking there would be plenty of time to relent. Hiding felt safe."

Emily paused and looked vulnerable. She smiled wistfully and sighed. I imagined she had momentarily dreamed herself off to a faraway parlour.

"And?" I interrupted.

"Safety never came," she said, "or rather, it arrived as a chance to study abroad. *That* was a choice I could embrace. I made the quest for art seem a wee bit more significant than it was at the time, so I could officially retreat and pine in peace. My wild head grew more daring with an ocean between us, and I daresay, the letters I sent Martyn had love woven into the margins. I was of two minds; we were of two opinions. He remained steadfast; I became more confused. One moment I was immovable, the next, willing. I was beastly to him.

Proximity to Martyn unnerved me, distance made me long for him and spin impossible stories. Eventually, the unnerving part shattered my dream and I physically crumbled. I called for him at night and shut him out in the day. Insomnia was excruciating and I became so agitated before bedtime that I was diagnosed with hysteria."

Emily blushed and fanned her face with a scented handkerchief. I smelled lavender waft from it as she continued.

"It's not real love if one remains calm. Hearts must bleed. Hysteria must be given its due. I got to play the 'femme collapse' card for all it was worth, and I played it so well and so often, it nearly finished me."

"Millie and Willie are a sublime rhyme," I remarked. "What infinite wordplay."

"How so?"

"M is the flip side of W. Both are followed by 'illie' – a meaningful literary echo. Will means power and a mill demands grist," I finished.

"You're not quite right in the head," Emily accused. "You have deciphered too many crossword puzzles. Cross words, indeed. Are you going to ask if you can tell Jon now and bring him to meet me?"

"I was g..."

"I will meet him later. When I say it's time. You can at least tell him that. Wait until I am steadier. For now, it has to be you and me... and Woo. Jon's advice and support will be invaluable in good time. Lean on that man. He is good for you."

"I shall consider the source."

"Hmph."

"Back to my remark about psychoanalysis being pointless," I said.

"It isn't," Emily chimed in, "there are reasons and excuses, but in the end it's human evolution that writes us and does us all in. No-one grows up in a vacuum. None of us. We are environ-mental-cases."

"I am a mental case for sure. Talking to you is not the act of a sane woman," I said.

"It's the act of an artist. One to another. One eccentric mind connecting perfectly with another. The chain of creativity, passed on."

I mimicked the dramatic performance of a flamboyant drummer and the sound-effects of a drum-riff punctuated with the climactic exclamation point of a crashing cymbal: Budda-bing-tish," I said.

Emily gaped.

"Miss Emily Carr has left the building," I declared. "She has truly passed on."

Emily looked piqued. It was a change from wounded, but not by much.

"But not annihilated," she added. "I've been waiting. Unfinished... potent. That's what creativity is. The art of living never dies. You and I... *we* are having a conversation," Emily said. "You're not channeling me, Scottie. This is not possession."

"Nine-tenths of the law says different. My one tenth demands a bottom-line. Miss Emily-ma'am. What do you want? Specifically!"

"What all spectres want Miss Watson. To right a wrong and dot some wayward i's, and be redeemed and saved, well... not saved, but affirmed. And to cross a few persistent detractors and t's... and... I've lost him," she finished, quite simply.

"That's a tall order. Perhaps you need a psychic investigator. Perhaps Jon is better suited to help you." I wanted to say ghostbuster, but the reference would have been lost, and in any event, she looked (pardon the expression) 'dead serious'.

"Let's use plain English, shall we? Love is already confusing enough," she said.

"You were in love. You thwarted, scuze me, rejected love. You have now chosen to travel back and accept? And I can help you... how?"

"No-one can travel back in time," Emily said.

"I think I know that," I said. "Then, how..."

"I need your legs."

"Okay."

"And your car."

Myriads of nurses
fluttering like white butterflies,
sisters as dignified as pine trees,
the gracious round-aboutness
of them spreading and ample.
One could never reach their hearts...
...I do not know my sister's name,
but she's beautiful and radiant.
She is young and straight and serene
standing there near the door.
Unless you need something,
she will not touch you,
and you would never dare
to put out your hand
to be touched.

~ Emily Carr ~
Hundreds and Thousands

*An immense love was offered to me
which I could neither accept
nor return.*

~ Emily Carr ~
Growing Pains

Preposterous Posthumous

"I was proper, but not prim," Emily began.

"Define prim."

"Stuffy, prudish."

"Define prude," I said.

"A prig."

"A chaste prig or a frigid prig?"

"I like you."

"So... frigid, then."

"Yes, but that's all changed."

"Do tell," I said, notebook poised like a reporter.

"The afterlife is not a repeat performance. One learns and progresses," Emily said, staring me down. "Do you see?"

"So, you're a wanton hussy again?"

"No, I was a naïve flirt who froze in shame. I have thawed. Now I'm a ... I'm proactive, but not *interactive*."

"And you want me to, what?... fix you up?"

"In a manner of speaking. I want to get married."

I was momentarily speechless, but I wanted to laugh. What a coup. Emily Carr was ready to exchange spinsterhood for marital bliss, and she needed a wedding planner. I'd finally gone loop-the-loop. I had nosedived down a rabbit hole of my own burrowing. No more mixed hallucinogens (antacids and indiscriminate curry) for me. Ever.

"I'm still surprised over your disclosure about the mystery tennis man you waxed so coy and desperate about in your memoirs?" I said, "what did he say?" It was impertinent, and I mentally prepared myself for a tongue lashing.

The verbal whipping never came. "I need you to find a grave," Emily said, meekly. It was a new Emily, and I pushed past her mild manner in my usual defensive mode.

"Oh joy," I said. "I'm not doing *that* kind of digging."

"I also need to know why a group of people..."

My sarcasm interrupted her. "Seven male artists in Ontario perhaps?" I interjected.

"This is serious, Scottie. A few *people* are preventing my progress. Some I can guess; not every entity progresses at the same speed. Anyway, it's not a *person's* grave I want you to find. Well, not at first. It's a cache of buried *things*. I was too feeble in my last stages of illness so I had someone else take care of them. Now I don't know where to look, and if I can't touch Martyn's letter I won't be able to find him. Signatures are critical tracking devices."

"A cache of paper in a shoebox will be mush by now," I said.

"No it won't. It's in a bank vault."

"That's harder. It requires an altogether different kind of shovel."

Emily had been adamant we meet in the cemetery and to penetrate my seeming ignorance, she repeated that she had to hold a *particular* letter in her hand. Martyn's signature was crucial. I had come to think of William and Martyn as interchangeable names. "Would a death certificate be enough?" I asked, "I can get my hands on a copy, no problem."

I received the look of sympathy at my ignorance. "Not his *name*. Not *typed*. His original *signature*. Not a copy of it. The actual ink and flesh impression left from skin on paper is required. The emotions linked to handwritten words capture the exact sentiments underlying the time of writing. Sometimes they contain a single tremble; other times, an entire symphony of mixed emotions. Will's given names on a cold contract won't do at all. It has to be fraught paper. We sent each other those; there are some left. Vital organic threads."

"Psychic DNA," I added, for my own clarification.

"Whatever *that* is," Emily said, "You see? I was being good. I left your mind alone for a second."

"Well, thanks," I said.

"We met here for a reason. There's good news and bad news," Emily announced, with her head to one side.

"Give me the bad news," I said.

Her form waivered slightly. "You will need to meet another ghost and tend my garden."

"Then the good news had better be fan-bloody-tastic," I said, "I hate gardening and, apart from yourself, I don't want to believe in a vast population of *interactive* dead people in need of favours."

"Her name is Regina." Emily gestured towards the furthermost eastern sector of the cemetery.

"She's somewhere over there in the Catholic paddock. She was a nun, my nurse. My little 'Poor Clare'."

"Ross Bay Cemetery is a regular floor puzzle of social discrimination," I commented.

"Regina disturbs me with her guilt. She can't see me or talk to me, she just rants and prays and as I already told you, she didn't bury the box as I asked. It plagues her, upsets me, and is playing havoc with my progress. Her sin is worse than my arthritis: I can't forgive her and she couldn't hear me if I did."

"She did you a favor," I said. "The earth is none too forgiving to cardboard and paper."

Emily ignored me. She looked like an empty dress blowing on a clothes line. "Within the missing box lies your coup of some juicy archive letters to auction," she taunted. "You will have some financial security. No-one knows better than I, how that makes a woman feel relevant. And, as an added incentive, I won't curdle the cream in your tea."

"You're doing it again. You have to stop reading my mind," I said, "It's uncomfortable."

"Honesty usually is. Curb your criticisms and judgements."

"That's like telling someone not to think of elephants."

Emily let out a guffaw, "oh girl... don't think of me standing at the foot of your bed tonight. Just say, yes..." I saw Emily pause and look up to her right, as if listening. "Sorry, *two* more ghosts," she added.

"And the good news?" I asked.

"Meeting Regina will be over in a couple of days," she replied. "You have to meet her on the anniversary of her death."

WooWoo VERONICA KNOX

The clothesline was almost empty and I returned to Jenner and my car. I was left with the kind of decision I didn't want to make. I am not a ghost-friendly sort of person. One is enough; one is too much. Multiple ghosts is over-the-top for me – the taxed non-believer with a dozen smart-ass philosophies and the 'don't waste my time' attitude, for delusional nutbars, gullible enough to swallow anything. New-Age Kool Aid was never on my menu.

If it weren't for Jon, I would still label anything remotely sixth sense as puerile tomfoolery, but Jon makes a compelling argument, and he has besozzzled me. He relates hours of lucid science which connects rationally to the unknown. Jon believes that quantum sensitivities, the laws of physics, and clairvoyance are art-forms with life-force.

How could I doubt a man who tells me these things with a Roberty voice and an Anthony face who calls me darling?

I called after the wavering flag that was Emily's disappearing tent-dress. "Okay, you win... fine... yes!" I turned for home, dragging an exhausted Jenner out of a nap, and prepared myself for ghost-napping duty, but first I would have to locate Emily's time capsule of guilt.

I heard Emily's voice echo in my head: "We can talk in our regular place, tomorrow. Same time as usual. What's a ghostbuster?"

"Great," I thought. "The woman will never stop playing games with my mind."

Father kept sturdy me
as his pet for a long time.
Ah, he would say,
this one should have been the boy.

~ Emily Carr ~
Growing Pains

Daddy's Girl

"It was the age of discipline," Emily said. "Children were neither seen nor heard until summoned to appear and perform."

"Like little monkeys," I said, teasing Woo with my pen.

"Yes. We stood to attention and were made to recite prayers and to sing for guests. Admonishments came with humiliating labels. I was considered a 'very naughty little maid'. That is what Papa called me, while Lizzie stood beside him, arms crossed, lips pursed, brows knitted into her own brand of spiteful authority."

It was an old story: Richard Carr wanted a son and coaxed Emily into playing the tomboy substitute until a son was born. She had been subtly groomed to fill the void of weakling boys who had died soon after birth. She had to be tougher and more daring than the household of daughters that Father Carr had co-created. It was no secret, although it was secretive, that Richard senior was a

Woo Woo VERONICA KNOX

cad who betrayed Emily's dream of paternal devotion. Woo turned bright red and began running in circles around Emily. "What did your father do to you," I asked.

"I suppose he was honest, even earnest, but it was too crude. My father assumed I was tough as a boy because I feigned boyishness from the start."

"A heyday for Freudians then," I said.

"I was the typical apple of a father's eye. He treated me like an adult, until he surpassed even *his* capacity for insensitivity, and shared too much."

"Birds and the Bees 101 – reproduction unplugged?" I suggested.

"It wasn't a joke, Scottie. It was a time when showing an ankle was tantamount to prostitution.

Mother wasn't there to soften the blow, and Lizzie was a harridan. Lizzie had been father's first *best little girl*, and I supplanted his memory of her. Mother died, and Dede had to grow up and play the role of surrogate mother and chatelaine. Lizzie never forgave me; as I never forgave him."

"The dynamics of siblings and power made your sister a tyrant, but she was a victim too. She fell into the same traps, surely?"

"She also set a few. I could do nothing right. She was the one who asked father to take me in hand about procreation. She pushed the lesson to its contemptible end."

"So, that was the 'Brutal Telling' that you were so evasive about?"

I could hardly embarrass my sensitive sisters. Father explained lust and the rudiments of mounting the female of any species to produce an heir. It was bestial farm talk, meant to illustrate, but it ruined my innocence with ghastly images of my father atop my fragile mother. It was not lost on me that he had impregnated her more than the nine times which produced his children. Many more. And... something else.

"He confided in you as his equal?"

"Mother was too ill to be a wife. Father had designs on another woman, the same age as his eldest daughter. He was proud of her and wanted one of us to know. He decided it would be me, and that I would visit her. Become friends."

"Did you go?"

"He tricked me into meeting her."

"Oh, Emily."

"I turned on him and his guilt took root. My disgust floored my father's plans of remarrying, and soon after his fancy woman met me, she left him. It was she *and* I who destroyed him. He didn't die of remorse over my mother, although he did miss her as was his duty. He died of rejection from his floozy, and me, his beloved 'Millie'. He was spurned the same way I have spurned every suitor who came too close, since."

"Even the ones you liked?"

"Even the one I loved!"

"Your father taught you well. No wonder you couldn't forgive him."

"My father distorted love. The world was reduced to a show of social lies – an Old Boys' dirty club. Two sets of rules: them and us. He polluted his gender into a rough heir-hungry mob with disgusting self-gratifying morals. He spoiled romance and maligned God. He killed the better part of my innocence. He explained the man's apparatus. Described its function. Its *hard* work, using examples of the animals which he knew I loved. He destroyed the illusions of sweet affection that I had clung to."

"Friction? Stimulation? Ejaculation?

"Yes. Yes. And, yes!"

"Did he abuse you?"

"Telling all was abusive enough. He spared me nothing."

"He never fondled or ... explored your... er... nether regions?"

"Have you entirely lost your mind!"

"Sorry, there's no discreet way to ask."

"Scottie! I was his *favorite* child! Was I jostled on his knee? Yes. Was I forced to kiss him at bedtime? Yes. Weren't those abuses of fatherhood enough?"

"I read how much you hated kissing his beard."

"He even believed himself cursed, which was why he attended church. He had bargained for a son. He had four too weak to live, and he told me how he hated God for that. He went to his own church so as to separate himself from Mother's God and my sister's piety. Their faith was nauseating, he said, and to top off his sorrow, my brother, Richard, was born to become a mama's boy, birthed like his brothers, sickly and not expected to live long."

Emily's male betrayals were mapped one-by-one, in puberty. Suitors arrived in a timely fashion, never failing to disappoint her low expectations. They spoke and acted out according to scripts of squeamish biology. No young men could be trusted for long, if at all. Senility set older men apart as acquaintance material, having burned off their sexual energies to embrace celibacy and intellectual pursuits.

Lizzie had dismissed Emily as a crude girl who promised to be a certain disgrace to the family. Betrayed by her instincts and curiosity, her sex and her dying mother, Emily endured relentless persecution from her sisters. She was broken like a wild horse, but at first, she resisted. Only later after constant criticism, did she begin (to her detriment) to believe in the system more than herself.

She was soon deprived of the first freedoms, bound into a corset to become a complacent prospective wife – a candidate for the slow death of matrimony or the swifter, 'death-by-motherhood'.

"I left my dance card on a scrapheap," she said. "Father died. Dede abdicated and Lizzie reigned."

"So, sister witch was in her element," I said.

"I left home to punish Lizzie. I wasn't courageous until much later. I left in a flutter of petticoats and tears."

"*That's my girl* is an endearment that really touches me," I confessed.

"For me it sounded more like *atta boy*."

"And so you chose independence as much as it was forced upon you?"

"I chose emancipation. I wanted male power and success and to keep my sexual fantasies, which were intense and frequent. There was pleasure to be had on the wings of imagination. Fantasy came easy to me," she said.

It was clear that Victorian women surrendered to the dehydration of spinsterhood in order to circumvent the alternative: to love amongst a suffocating forest of men that choked out the sunlight and sucked out freedom. Marriage equaled twice the freedom for the husband after he usurped his wife's and lorded it over his subservient offspring. The few feisty daughters who rebelled were determined to remain unconquered, intact, and precious. Maternal instincts brewed as they have since the beginning of procreation. Men couldn't compete with motherhood, but neither was pregnancy romantic. By logical progression, one married and the inevitability of childbirth ensued. According to Emily, matrimony was basically an act of suicide.

"I blossomed with wallflower innocence," Emily confided. "It was heaven for a while – sublime fears panicking under pounding joy. I relished the suspended moment of crossing a room, of eye contact, the blush at first sight, and the sweet trickle of love beginning to flow. Liquid gold spilling down one's spine."

"Steady on girl," I said. The teenage Emily before me, was sixteen going on thirty, "I didn't know you could be so graphic."

Young Emily bristled. "What do you think I *burned*?" she said, "Recipes?"

It is not all bad,
this getting old, ripening.
After the fruit has got its growth
it should juice up and mellow.
God forbid I should live long enough
to ferment and rot
and fall to the ground
in a squash.

~ Emily Carr ~

We but level this lift
to pass and continue beyond.

~ Walt Whitman ~
Song of Myself

Dearly Beloved

I addressed my wandering thoughts and bid them come close and listen. I wanted to begin with: *recently departed, we are gathered here together, in order to make sense of some extremely disturbing developments.* But I merely asked them to rest quietly and listen without interrupting, and let them know there would be a question and answer period following my latest plan. It's called internal brainstorming.

Emily had blocked out Martyn's love with fear, putting distance between them by going to England to study art. His earnest attentions terrified her. She questioned her right to receive praise. The Carr sisters had done their worst to achieve a lasting sense of artistic inadequacy. Emily's paintings were false, they quipped, embarrassing abominations. Emily smoked and cursed, she was going to the devil in a hand cart, fast.

Decades later, even the *Group of Seven* would seem like a cruel boy's club at times. Emily said sometimes they seemed more like an optical illusion of camaraderie rather than new friends? When her first public recognition came, it was almost accepted by proxy.

If Emily had employed an agent, she would have retreated to the shadows. Some podium excuse: *The real Emily couldn't be here tonight to accept this award. She was unavoidably detained by a monkey, a parrot and a griffon... no, seriously folks...*

Woo acted as Emily's mood ring. Today she was dark brown wearing basic black eye shadow. "I'm not molecular; I'm unrestricted," Emily spat. "Creative. I occupy no space other than time. I was once here and now I'm here in a more intensive form."

"Yes," I agreed. "You have a haunting personality."

Emily was playing the harpy in an over-the-top performance. "If I were haunting you, you would know it Madame! I'm reaching out. Is that so hard to digest? So scary?"

"Emily my dear, your press is scary."

"I did something right then," she said, softening to the consistency of granite.

I reacted, equally flinty, and made reference to putting recent events in better perspective.

"Don't '*dearie*' me," she scolded. "You think being dead isn't the ultimate definition of perspective?"

"I can't think of anything more enlightening," I said.

"How about a dead person's hindsight? You can call them warnings or hauntings, but they're some of the best advise anyone is ever likely to receive."

"And demands," I said. "It was always your way or no way, José."

"I paid for my obstinacies. I earned the right to be persnickety," she said. "Who is José?"

"I am *so* lucky."

Rainy days invigorate me. Drops danced on the top of my umbrella in the delightful timpani percussion of a love song. It was time to confess. Emily had given me permission.

The James Bay Tearoom was bustling with afternoon customers. The steamy asteroid's tea and crumpet civilization murmured to each other through an atmospheric haze of exotic Lapsang Souchong and Oolong. The scent of Jasmine misted the stained-glass windows.

Jon was there, at the best table, nearest the fireplace, a fat teapot already waiting with Earl Grey. The fusion of well-steeped bergamot and Darjeeling greeted me pleasantly as he poured for one.

"I've ordered watercress sandwiches (crusts removed), scones, clotted cream and raspberry jam," he said, shyly. I was flattered and impressed. A cream tea is a thing of beauty on a damp day.

I struggled with my words. "This is lovely, thank you." It sounded feeble considering what I had come to divulge.

"You look serious. I meant to cheer you up. It's our anniversary. Four whole weeks."

"Dear Jon," I began, and blushed. It sounded like a letter of rejection.

"Not goodbye already," he said, with a crooked smile. "If it's the wrong jam I can order marmalade. I checked, they have Robertson's Golden Shred."

I stare into his hurt puppy eyes and offered a treat. "No, no, I'm biding my words for the right moment. I fear you are contagious."

"That was my devious plan."

"Your theories... um... I've had an... I *may* have

had an... *encounter.* Way past my comfort zone and well into your... area of expertise."

"Which one, Mademoiselle? I am at your service."

I saw him relax and I felt slightly guilty. "It's very 'woo woo'. I refer of course to your haunting abilities of probing beyond the veil," I said, staring into the center of his pupils till he was out of focus. It was obvious Jon was drawn to me and I to him, but he was out in the open, and I hid behind business as usual.

"Come on in," he said, "the zone's fine."

"Well, I can't swim."

"I will save you," he said, and I relaxed. I imagined strong arms compassionately taking my weight, and although we were across from each other, separated by the width of a deep table, I felt I was leaning on a familiar shoulder.

I surrendered to his hypnotic powers. "I've met a ghost... I *may* have met a ghost. Barring either of those, I've gone mad. I prefer to think it's the first."

Jon searched my eyes for the joke, but my intense stare must have convinced him of my sincerity. He spooned the foam off his latte and smiled. "If you have, you're a lucky girl. Consider me besotted, riveted, and impressed... in that order. Spill."

There was the exact same word I had used tongue in cheek: lucky. Had I suddenly become lucky? Was it luck that propelled me into the spotlight of a supernatural stalking. I hoped it meant that I had finally become lucky in love.

My Emily experience engaged Jon beyond his usual attentive manner. He was thrilled. Thrilled for me and for us, as we were sharing the strange encounter. Bonding was all important to a man intent on making an honest woman of me. His position was sincere. He didn't fawn all over me with gratuitous interest. He was truly absorbed, and not one doubt darkened our tea date. He had theories.

Jon's face was that of a small boy saying 'yes, please' to an ice-cream cone dipped in sprinkles. His eyebrows were raised expectantly "Do you want me to go with you?" he asked.

How could I tell him about Emily's decision? I had thought that blood was thicker than ectoplasm, but I had been wrong. Emily and Woo were in control. The waitress must have got my order wrong and brought me Gunpowder tea, because my next words blasted Jon's immediate hopes for a ghostly rendezvous together:

"Jon, I'm so sorry. Emily said no. She said on no account were you to come. I'd better go alone until Emily gives permission. Miss Emily is likely to have an apoplectic fit, if that's possible after one has already died from heart failure."

Jon's face was the ground-zero of disappointment, but he was not devastated. He thought for a moment and became the practical ghostician. "No, it's okay," he said. "We don't want to lose her."

"Or tick her off," I said. "I really don't want to do that."

"Why? Does she turn green and burst out of her clothes?"

"No, Woo does that for her," I said. "Imagine an irate monkey and multiply that by a hundred. It isn't pretty."

"I would pay to see that."

I glanced at the bill and waved it across the teapot. "It will cost exactly twelve dollars and ninety-two cents plus tip," I said.

"Never take wooden nickels from a green monkey," he said.

I had to agree. It was sound advise. That's when I knew for sure I loved him.

"What if I drove you there and waited in the Ross Bay Pub across the street?" he suggested.

"That would be such a relief. I wouldn't be long, and afterwards we could have supper. They serve the best Yorkshire Pudding tower thing."

"Thing? It sounds dubious."

"I have to say, it *looks* dubious when you first see it, but it tastes wonderful. It's the gravy. You can't fake good gravy, and we waxed on about the pros and cons of savoury sauces and the distinct advantage of onion as opposed to garlic for a good roast beef au jus.

For some strange reason I had gotten a chill when Jon mentioned marmalade, and I knew it was something that mattered to Emily. Something which set her on edge, so maybe she had been with us after all, as Jon premised. I intuited she probably left because of the reference to oranges.

Somewhere there is a beautiful place.
I went there again last night
In my dreams.
I have been there many, many times.

~ Emily Carr ~
Hundreds and Thousands
1937

Regina

n the 1970's, St Ann's Academy, the former convent, was sold to the City of Victoria, and the graves of the sisters buried behind the chapel were exhumed and moved to Ross Bay Cemetery. It was called a clean-up.

The replanted 'Poor Clares' of St. Ann's fared no better than the Carrs, but I had no calm expectations on my third visit to the graveyard. The names on the markers had been erased by rain and windy fingers that blew wildly across the Juan de Fuca Strait, many were finally toppled by vandals. The devastated corner looked like the foundations of a lost city, recently uncovered by archaeologists. The elegant white symmetry of Flanders Field was missing.

All I could do, was to meander and let Regina come to me. I strolled down a lane of grey mausoleum accommodation. A few ostentatious attempts of one-upmanship had sprouted between lesser mortal's, bleak apartments. Row-housing for the common man, vacation crypts for getting away from it all – a pastoral retreat from city-bound, hell. I hoped there was a heaven for their sakes.

I found myself walking back to Emily's graveside – the starting square on a macabre board game.

As far as ghosts go, Regina wasn't so bad. I had dreaded a shivering melancholic white vapor floating through the tombstones with a list of apologies – I was rooting for a benign levitating white sheet with two black eyeholes.

She was a sad, skinny girl, thin as an apparition should be, in a nun's habit, standing over Emily's grave like the ghost of Nurses Past. I almost quoted the line from Dickens: *Are you the spirit that was foretold to me*, but I stayed silent and let her speak first, too intimidated to be my normal, smart-mouth, self.

The waters of paranormal introduction were still muddy and I had no rational opening line. I thought of slipping away, not unlike a spectre myself, but my shoes made a crunch in the twig-strewn grass.

I froze: perhaps she hadn't heard me. Who knew if ghosts were sensitive to the sounds of life? The thought of Jon waiting across the street in a warm lively restaurant gave me courage.

The girl paused and spoke without facing me. "My name is Sister Valentina," she said.

"I am here to meet Regina. Have you seen her?" Making polite conversation was all I had left.

"That's me," she said. "I was formerly Regina," she continued, pronouncing it 'ray-jeena'. Her words slid over her shoulder as she spoke to the ground. "I need to speak with the lady buried here."

She raised her bowed head to engage me and I was relieved. Her eyes were a friendly human-brown, not the empty sockets of an ancient corpse, neither was her face a gaunt skull. My anxiety settled into curiosity.

She spoke in a list of confession like a practiced nun: "I failed her. I lied. I was wrong. I broke my promise. I read her letters. Tell her I'm sorry. Tell her Regina Watson is sorry."

Until she mentioned that her last name was Watson, the ground seemed solid.

"God!" I thought, quite irreverently: "the loose ends we do weave."

Valentina stared down at my shoes. "My fiancé died at sea before we could marry, and I took the veil."

"I'm so sorry. Is he buried here?" I asked, stupidly.

"It was necessary," she said... "I was with child."

I spared a quiet thought for the corporeal Regina, trapped in the family way with her nearest and dearest pushing her out of their way. Saving face; saving grace. I imagined a waif of a girl grieving in nine kinds of pain, seeking asylum in any quarter, finally reaching the end of her desperate road on the doorstep of Saint Ann's. Suicide couldn't have been far from her mind. Then love for her unborn child intervened to offer a reason to live.

Fallen girls back then, had little recourse. Flouting society held no cachet for women of any class. The tar brush was just as cruel to well bred girls as the common promiscuous ones. Feathers stuck to rich and poor alike.

"My stillborn child isn't buried here either," Regina said. "It was not permitted. My second child lived two days."

"Second?" I responded, shocked.

Regina hesitated, "What is your name?"

Reluctantly, I answered. I gave her Alba, which was the truth.

Regina spoke with hesitation. "I left the convent and ran to the streets, Alba. I lasted a couple of years before I knew I had to return to the service of God and repent for good."

Hearing a ghost say one's name is not the upbeat thrill one might imagine. "Miss Emily Carr sent me," I said. "She believes you desire to speak with me. She knows about the box," I told her. "Not burying it saved her letters and she is grateful to you, but I need to know where you left it. It was a bank, yes?"

Regina looked distraught. "I lost the key. I'm so very sorry."

"It's okay. You're not in any trouble," I said. "You did well. You saved Miss Carr's things."

Regina started to cry. "Please help me Alba," she begged. "Pray for me."

"You can call me Scottie," I said, "all my friends do."

We talked about heaven and I told her about tunnels and white lights, and I followed Regina as she wandered back to her own neighborhood, where she melted into the statue of Saint Clare, the patron saint of television (no kidding!) and I am pleased to report that she seemed happier after our conversation.

Woo Woo VERONICA KNOX

I played with the thought of Regina stuck in the past, and later wrote the words *poor Clare* and *Clair-voyance* in my notebook. I assumed Regina had located me with a need to cleanse herself of guilt rather than to deliver an unselfish message to save a pair of lovers she barely knew. She had remained estranged from her dearly beloved departed children and husband-to-be. I hoped she could move on and let them find her.

I jingled the car keys in my pocket from nervous habit to ground myself, and I encountered a small loose object. It was a flat brass key that I instantly knew would fit Emily's lost deposit box.

You must habit yourself
to the dazzle of the light
and of every moment of your life.

~ Walt Whitman ~
Song of Myself

The Rest is Gravy

The pub was noisy, and the tall booth Jon had chosen kept us isolated. He was expectant – more than relieved to see me. His eyes glowed like candles.

I slipped onto the seat opposite him. "Emily wasn't there," I said.

Jon's eyes stayed bright. "But Regina was?"

"She was. She really was."

"You need a drink?"

"Double brandy," I said to the waitress.

Jon leaned forward and took my hand. "That's my girl," he said, and turned to the woman taking our order. "I'll have a Johnny Walkers Special Old, neat."

I blushed and straightened the cutlery. I wanted to be Jon's girl, and I could see he had meant it literally and not as an automatic praise for.... for what? ordering a big-girl's drink?

Jon's face lit up the dark corner. Menus arrived, and I ordered the house special, Stuffed Yorkie, the dish I had promoted so adamantly.

"Make that two," Jon said. "What's good enough for the goose is good enough for the gander."

"It won't disappoint," I said.

"But will your encounter?"

I slid over to his side of the table and he put his arm around me. I forgot my ghostly news and surrendered until he nudged me.

"Come on, tell all. What happened? Can I go next time? Did Emily give her permission?"

"I told you, Emily wasn't there. Two spectres would have been too much like ganging up on a single mortal."

"I bet sure as hell she was watching. She knows what happened."

"A fly on the wall?" I joked.

"What now?"

"I call on Miss Carr," I said.

"Game on!" he announced, rubbing his hands together.

My face fell in shock. "That's the attitude that will curdle Emily's disposition. She is *deadly* serious, most of the time. Always, when it's about Martyn."

Jon laughed, "Lighten up sweetheart."

His remark rankled me. I hated that expression. "Emily doesn't have a sense of humor about whatever is troubling her... and as you say, she probably knows already."

"She could be in this bar," Jon said, impressed with the notion.

He lifted his glass to an empty chair. "To you Miss Carr. Very pleased to meet you."

I was about to reply, but two plates bearing small active volcanoes of raised pastry stuffed with shaved roast beef arrived, swaying on beds of mashed potato, pouring lava gravy down the sides, and we were distracted.

"So much for presentation," he said. "It looks like a science project I built in grade six."

"Let's hear it for brandy and gravy," I said.

Jon raised his glass, to me this time: "And savvy," he said. "You are one brave kid."

"Well, I told you I didn't believe in ghosts."

"I can read you deeper than that," he whispered. "You were scared. That spells courage in my dictionary. To spirit and spirits."

"Shut up and eat your volcano," I said.

*It is rather wonderful to
get a Christmas letter
from a man who loved you
forty years ago.*

~ Emily Carr ~
Hundreds and Thousands
1936

Thinking Inside the Box

t was easy to assemble an accurate genealogy. I had contacts who specialized in such information, so after I read the fax that confirmed Regina Watson was my ancestor, the project became less bizarre. My theories of inherited memories covered all the logical bases. I was linked to Emily by a familial calling to free a wretched girl. I carried some residual responsibility for a girl who had been an obscure second cousin of my mother's great aunt. Perhaps it had even been my mother's spirit who had alerted Emily. I didn't actually want to know.

I approached the Bank of Montreal clerk, presentation in hand, and she passed me to a lackey with his very own cubicle. As he perused the documents I glanced at his impressive display of rubber stamps and tried to look nonplussed. I knew there would be a cavernous desk drawer in which he kept an endless roll of red tape in the unlikely event he was unable to sniff out enough in his current assignment.

In my line of work, I came across these half-way-executives all the time. Their sentences inevitably opened with 'I'm sorry, but' and after making one wait, came to the 'I wish I could help', and always concluded with 'I'm afraid there's nothing I can do'.

In due course he laid down my paperwork, faked a cheery no problem look and announced, "I'm sorry, but..."

His verdict? It would take several months of paperwork to verify my claim, unless I could produce in triplicate the birth and death certificates of the deceased and every document in between which connected us.

I related my day over homemade spaghetti sauce. I stirred and Jon listened. "It wasn't a no," I said, "but the delays will push the patience of Miss Carr. I can't face her without a plan B."

I watched Jon's expression transform from sympathy to amazement, as he refilled my wineglass and pressed it into my hand. His eyes glinted with mischief. "Tell me again," he said. His face was about to burst. "Would you say the situation was grave? Sorry, please start from the bank part. Where did you say the box is?"

"It's in the Bank of Montreal on Fort," I repeated. "They said no way. Why are you grinning? If you've got a plan let's hear it."

"I'm laughing because I was waiting for something like this to happen. Things weren't tidy. They didn't make sense. There are rules of paranormal priority. I was involved in your mission, but I was shut out. Now I know where I fit. Now it makes perfect sense."

"Well I'm still in the dark. Can you light a candle or something."

"My father manages that bank."

"Jon! That's incred..."

"He hates me," Jon cut in.

"Terrible," I finished.

"But I do know how to get into the safety deposit vault. His secretary will do anything for me."

"Including stealing from her bank?"

Jon's enthusiasm was evident. "No, including helping my cousin Alba open a deposit box to add some items. We take one shoebox in and take the original box out. She is easily distracted."

"Not too swift then."

"Not as such."

"Okay," I said, alarm bells ringing in the distance.

"Dad doesn't work on Mondays."

"So?"

"Trudi does."

"Trudi without the e?" I say in my best breathless dumb-blonde voice.

"The same," he said.

Trudi *was* blonde. Not the buxom cutie I imagined, but a statuesque beauty who looked through me during our introduction. Jon had the same effect on her as a stage hypnotist. She was a goner. Jon held her attention the way a cobra psyches out a rabbit. I didn't want to watch.

I wanted to test Trudi's trancelike state just to show her up as a dim bulb. Petty, I know, but beautiful supermodels threaten me, especially now that I have a Ghostbuster Ken to mate with their Swimsuit Barbie.

I was introduced to the door of the bank vault. "Intrudi alert," I said to Emily, who had shifted into her huffy disdainful persona. Jon gave me a look that had nothing to do with hypnotism.

Trudi and Jon chatted about old times for the prerequisite reminisce while I waited with Emily, and Trudi continued to ignore me, even when I said: "Who do you have to sleep with around here to get into a deposit box?" in a loud stage whisper.

Jon kicked my foot. I got *the look,* twice. He was in danger of cracking up.

"Play nice," Emily growled at me. "Green is a bad color on you."

"I'm wearing black," I sent to Emily as a thought, and stared straight at Jon as Trudi collected the key to the vault. "Ya know, you can spell Trudeeeee with five 'e's? I said, tilting my head to one side and widening my eyes like Betty Boop.

Emily scowled at me and I shrugged an apology.

"Scottie with five e's," she hissed. "Don't mess about. This is my life."

I raised my eyebrows to make a snide remark.

"Yes, *life,* Miss High-horse," she said, waggling an arthritic finger in my face.

Meanwhile, back in the cemetery... but no, Miss Carr had consented to visit my flat in the very building which once housed her in ill health. St. Joseph's Hospital is now St. Joseph's Apartments where I live on the second floor. I prayed it didn't have memories to eclipse our mission. The box was on the coffee table – a work of art on a pedestal, and we sat around it like cats staring down a mouse.

The introductions had been so ordinary I was

disappointed. Jon took a back seat and kept quiet. He was watching a movie rather than being a cast member and I loved him for it. I had been worried he was going to go super-science, but he was all laid-back diplomacy. The normal rules followed the paranormal rules and dictated respect. Professionalism vs. Spiritualism: apparently it's a real thing.

Emily was silent for once.

"Open it," Jon encouraged. He was addressing me.

I looked to Emily for permission and met an expression that would frighten a grizzly into retreat. Jon had backed away to the window and was behind her, so he missed the Medusa face that challenged me.

Emily's silence was permission enough and I opened the lid stuck down with ancient cellotape, so yellowed and brittle that it crumbled as soon as it was disturbed.

What may one expect? It was a box of documents and a few keepsakes. It wasn't releasing a genie from a bottle. I comforted myself, silently, "There won't be a sudden swoosh of magical energy with folded arms," I told myself and was reassured. No cloud of bats. No puff of Disney fairy dust; however, an image of a Woo with blue fur wearing a fez and a miniature Aladdin's costume (a là an organ-grinder's shill) came to mind. I was rigid with expectation.

In a movie, the phone would ring and the tension would disintegrate. I glanced at my landline. Once again the receiver was off the hook of its own accord. Okay, it was getting spooky. But then, how could it not?

Holding everything down was a shape wrapped

in tissue. I placed it on the table and started to empty the box. The next item was a bundle of letters tied in blue ribbon.

Emily pounced, "that is what I've come to see," she said, as she grabbed them greedily. The mute spell over her was clearly broken. She attacked the ribbon with old shaking fingers as I closed the lid on the rest of the contents.

We watched Emily work the knot under the bow. I couldn't help thinking about the dead letter department of the post office. Not surprisingly, the ribbon surrendered. It slipped through the trembling fingers of (a now young) Emily.

The letters were laid in two piles. One tall and in danger of toppling; the other consisting of three envelopes. "I asked him to return my letters," Emily said apologetically. It wasn't hard to guess which stack was from Martyn.

"Check the dates, they should be in order," Emily demanded. Her corresponding return letters indicated gaps of years between them. The last one had no stamp. Emily gasped and slumped into a chair with the envelope clutched in her hand. Jenner moved behind me, tail between his legs and whimpered. I knew something was wrong, but Emily refused to speak. Silent as the grave.

Jon braved Emily's wrath and coaxed her into a conversation.

"This is my last letter," Emily said, offering it to Jon. "It shouldn't be here. It was important to have sent it," she whispered. "Martyn promised on pain of death to wait."

Martyn had written his own last letter and Emily told us how she had been too upset to write back immediately. I could see she felt the power emanating from the ink when she held her hand over Martyn's signature.

Emily returned to her form as an old woman and Woo was uncharacteristically subdued. "I dawdled and eventually drafted a reply and I must have forgotten to post it, so Martyn never received it. It was imperative I answered that last time. It was the link to us meeting again. I'm a damned fool."

I could see the headlines: 'Marriage called on account of hesitation'. "Why Emily? Why was is it, so important? What's in a name?"

"It's what's in a *signature*," Emily insisted. "They hold an echo of life – a mere scratch of such energy is enough. That letter was our last contact. Paper is receptive. Emotions are imprinted energy signatures that seep into the surface. Messages handled by us held our energy intact."

"But, Regina read it. She touched it."

"She read some, maybe not this one, and her energy was too low to disrupt ours. I can feel that. That one was sent from Martyn to me inside a protective shell. Our energies merged from his hand to mine. My letter would have sealed the message like a fly in amber."

"Emily!" Jon's voice was firm the way an ambulance attendant speaks to an accident victim in shock. "Listen to me. There is always a way around things, as impossible as they may seem. I need you to tell me why you're meeting is compromised. I promise, I will help you."

Amazingly, Emily smiled at Jon and said, "thank you." For now, a man had been put in charge of a couple of unable-to-cope women. I was relieved. Jon was being wonderful. Emily ignored me and spoke directly to Jon. She sighed, turned away from me and began. Jon's face was enraptured. I watched them like a scene from a surreal movie.

"I wanted to tell you afterwards as a surprise," I said to Emily. Martyn's grave has been located."

Emily tried to smile. "Thank you Scottie, you worked hard."

"It's in San Diego."

"It's unimportant now. It's too late."

"Maybe not," I said, and looked over to Jon for help.

Jon had been mulling quietly for some time. Thankfully, he walked over and interrupted my feeble attempt to console Emily. "I think I may have a solution," he said, "hear me out."

"How in heaven?" I started to protest.

"Precisely, darling. The staid laws of physics can't possibly apply here. However, the laws of metaphysics is fluid. It seems to me, Emily, that you can complete that broken link by signing your original draft. We will simply mail it. Just forget the date."

"Bit of a long shot, then," Emily said.

"It's a shot," Jon countered. "C'mon Emily. Let's give it a try."

"Can't hurt," came the ambivalent reply.

"Jon knows about these things," I added, with misgiving. Jon smiled and made a writing gesture in the air over Emily's head, for me to get a pen. I kept my face away from Emily and retrieved one from my desk. Jenner trotted close to my heels and wouldn't return to the living room.

"How will we know?" I asked the room.

"I'll know," Emily said with conviction. "I will know. Woo will tell me."

It was easily done. Signed and sealed in a heartbeat. "Emily must be the one to mail it," Jon insisted. "Let's not take any chances." The three of us shuffled off to the corner where the red guardian of snail mail waited. Woo took the opportunity to let out her pent up frustration and disappeared over the convent wall.

I had done freakier things, but nothing so melodramatic. One expects fireworks overhead from the psychic gluing of a ripped tear in time. I said as much and Jon squeezed my shoulder. "True words are always spoken in jest," he said, and kissed the tip of my nose.

I didn't want Emily to see us. It was insensitive considering her present situation. I needn't have fretted. She was now across the street looking up at a weeping willow in St. Ann's old orchard. I could see a green shape dangling from a long strand of leaves swinging towards the earth. Emily was underneath it, encouraging a small pale-green Woo to come down. "Jump," she commanded, and Woo dropped like a stone onto her arm.

Woo and Emily appeared beside us again, and Woo began to hop madly on top of the mailbox. Woo had turned to Autumn. Her fur was a brighter shade of emerald, she wore an orange dress with a yellow belt and a red fez, I think to spite me my imaginative portrayal earlier. My mind was an open book to Emily and Woo. Their selectivity kept me surprised. Woo took the fez from her head and spun it a few times by its gold tassel before lobbing it in my direction.

"The energy has changed. It has settled," Emily declared. "Woo, come here you little monkey."

Woo leaped onto Emily like a flea, and flung her arms about her neck.

"Minx," I said, handing Woo her flower-pot-shaped hat.

"We haven't been formally introduced," Jon said, holding a finger out to Woo. "I'm Jon. Miss Woo I presume," he said, in a soothing voice. Woo hugged Jon's finger and cooed like a dove.

After the momentous posting ceremony, the contents of the box seemed an anti-climax, but at first, it served to pacify Woo. Emily let monkey fingers examine each treasure. Woo unrolled the tissue paper and hugged the small ivory elephant within. It was beautifully crafted, trunk up for good luck – her totem pal, Jumble, who had been her consort on so many occasions of prophecy. Next came a hair-net. A whole hairnet. *The* hairnet.

"I knew it was a hairnet and not a headband," I said, but as my words were still warm, Woo pulled out a black headband and threw it in my face. A double find that could be confirmed with DNA. The familiar brown photograph of the tennis party was crisp as new, but torn in half. The Emily side broadcasted a sense of futility that I hadn't caught back in the 'lab'. Lastly, underneath all, was one of Woo's flannel dresses. A saucy red number, flat as a pressed rose.

WooWoo VERONICA KNOX

I knew what Emily was thinking: she was reading my mind and I was reading it too. My thoughts were shameful: *'I don't need you now. I've got your love letters, a priceless hairnet (DNA included) and a bonus red monkey's dress,'* it said.

"It's not nice to fool Mother Nature," Emily replied.

"It's my dark side," I said, "there's nothing I can do about it. It's doing its devil's advocate thing. I have no control over it."

"Yes," Emily said, "it's wise to remember that Woo is in control."

I started to feel queasy.

Emily addressed Jon and I: "Now it's time for both of you to read a couple of books," she said, "they will help you focus."

Emily's order came as a relief. How hard could it be for an avid reader? But, like all things Emily, it was a challenge. The books were bodice-rippers penned by the Victorian Queen of paranormal romance herself, Miss Marie Corelli.

Woo climbed to my curtain rod and tenderly stroked Jumble the elephant, while Dolly and Lucozade stayed under my bed. The energy of the love-letters had travelled as fast as an e-mail. E for Emily; M for Martyn.

Why do inexplicable sadnesses
suddenly swell up inside one,
aching sadness over nothing in particular?

~ Emily Carr ~
Hundreds and Thousands

The Corelli Factor

had unsuccessfully rifled through my captain's trunk coffee table in search of the 'Marie books' that had belonged to my mother, even though I was one hundred percent sure I'd thrown them away. Instead, I found Marmie. I kept her out to show Jon and closed the lid on nostalgia.

I told Emily I couldn't find the books, and therefore the passages, that were meant to enlighten me were unavailable.

Emily was adamant and not a little annoyed. "Read Marie again," she commanded. "This time, pretend it's science, because it is."

"I have no books by any Marie," I said. "What do you mean by, again?"

Emily made an impatient sound and glared at me with disdain. "Go back and check your shelves." She turned her back on me, thought better of it, and shooed me away.

"Go! Don't skulk, girl. I can't abide dawdlers."

"I only have a handful of books. I sold most of them to move here, so I know th..."

"Gracious girl! Your *shelves*! You work in libraries for heaven's sake! Well? Do you or don't you?"

"I do," I said sheepishly, "I never thought."

Martyn's grave had been easy to find online. So were Marie's books when I decided to really look for them. I was surprised to find her books were still active in the library system and immensely popular. They were so active they were signed out, but a second-hand bookstore came up trumps with both titles.

I took one look at them and realized Emily had been right. I recognized the book covers. It had been ten years since my mother had passed the same novels to me with her stamp of recommended reading. I had been forced to read them in a black funk of reluctant obedience to quell an argument. It had been a case of in one eye and out the other.

My mother had read that true love would arrive unexpectedly out of the blue, and she lived on the day-to-day hope that any moment her soul mate would appear. She had tried to instill this in me, the forever realist ahead of my time, but I was not a chip off the old block; I had a large skeptical boulder on my shoulder, big as a monkey, and I had hotly declared that I would never be a Pollyanna for love.

A Romance of Two Worlds and *The Life Everlasting* by Marie Corelli, were decidedly melodramatic love stories. Now I recoiled from reading them again in my present state of grown-up dignity. I had reached the hard-won plateau of maturity, and wasn't about to descend into girlish simpering. When I was a teenager, it had been amusing to hear of my grandmother's time and women's noses pressed into lavender hankies, swooning over erotic minutia. Now it had become pathetic to think of such a retrograde branch of feminine intelligence, brainwashed by imposed morality.

And then I remembered my ongoing fascination with the old prints in the archives of the genteel garden party creatures in the hats and gowns who beckoned to me with there awkward stares. I felt chastised. I had wished this very opportunity on myself. There I was, being invited to learn from a firsthand source, and I was hung up on metaphysical semantics.

Making a promise to an impatient ghost was intimidating and the repercussions were grim enough for me to immediately address the yellowed pages of a book printed in 1866.

I have learned the art of scanning written material. Research eyes sweep blocks of text for keys. No-one knows more than I, that to read for content one has to concentrate. I have to separate myself from the world to read reclusive themes. It's like diving. I have a full tank of time devoted to sunken treasure. I swim over bedrock text for the glint of gold. There isn't time for distractions. In this case it was a mass of plots and superfluous literary filler, worse than a coral reef choked with seaweed.

Research missions are goal specific. In a novel choked with flamboyant language I had to ignore every segue of Victorian melodrama and focus. Emily's 'science' lay underneath a ton of debris, but the only way past her quest was through the deal we made. I resigned myself to a humiliating search.

Jon took Jenner for a long walk while I made tuna-fish sandwiches, arranging them on two platters with an assortment of cookies and grapes. I cleared the coffee table and set each end with water and wine glasses and paper serviettes. Then I fed the cats to discourage their curiosity for the human food placed so tantalizing within reach. I piled Marie's novels in the center. One was a paperback edition with a small font, the other a hardcover that appeared deceptively twice the size.

As I fixed a bowl of kibble and rice for Jenner, I heard his faint bark from across the street. I joined Dolly and Luke at the window and waved to Jon below. The plan had been to wear Jenner out so Jon and I could read uninterrupted for a couple of hours, food and drink to hand, comfortable enough to settle in and nap in situ if need be.

The plan worked, Jenner dived into his water bowl and slurped for a long time in dog minutes, then collapsed on his bed where he sprawled into an exhausted sleep.

"That's what I want to do," Jon said, looking at him. "We had quite a workout, but I'll do my best to accommodate Emily. Where's the wine and those ghastly books?"

I made made the sofa cosy with extra pillows and throws while Jon opened a bottle of Pinot Noir. When I went to take the phone off its hook, someone had beaten me to it.

"Seagull, did you take the phone off the hook?" I called from the bedroom.

"It happened again?" Jon called back. "Cool." Phone acrobatics were getting to be a regular event that belied the normal in paranormal.

Jon selected a title and poured the wine. "I'm taking the little one," he said, "you're the professional reader. We can exchange if we need to in an hour or so."

"If only it were that easy," I said.

We burrowed into our reading nest, positioning ourselves to face each other with our legs intertwined. Dolly curled into my arm, and I programmed my brain to seek the words love, death, soul, mate, and reincarnation. Lucozade made himself comfortable on Jon's lap. We each claimed a receptive space - our wine and snacks within reach.

"Here's what I see right away," Jon said, tapping the front cover of his book, "the name Marie appears inside the name Marmie."

"Corelli," he pronounced slowly, separating the three syllables. "Core really, the real core. What we're trying to find," he said. "Yes. I like it."

I broke the seal of history, eased open the musty pages of the hard copy, and sniffed. Now I know what time smells like. I half expected to see a spidery dedication from Emily's eldest sister, Dede, to Lizzie on the frontispiece.

I took a sip of wine and let its fruity chill trickle down my throat. Jon was already popping grapes into his mouth and turning pages and had settled on the midway point of the book in his hand, not a fortuitous place to start, but I was happy he was with me. I didn't have the heart to tell him to begin with the foreword. His company was enough. Jon alternately fussed Lucozade and massaged my toes as he read. We skimmed, but there was no immediate sign of cream, just a thick scum of romantic codswollop swirling on the top of some obscure scientific phenomenon. Jon had no idea what he was in for.

I had originally pooh-poohed Miss Corelli's inspirational messages with the crisp logic of a next generation's arrogance, and my mother had smiled sadly. "Even if you're so sure I'm wrong, why deny yourself the fantasy?" she had said. "You are young. Love is a promise made in heaven." I had replied scathingly that I didn't believe in heaven. And she had replied back: "not the church one, but the soul one." It had been futile to point out they were the same thing. She went on to explain that reincarnation hid the obvious in order to be fair.

My parent's marriage had been one of convenience until my father abandoned us. It had been a blind date gone horribly wrong. I believed that the romantic theories of revived spiritualism were a crutch for desperate women, and I told her so. My mother replied that she had come to terms with not finding her soul mate in this life, but nonetheless, was excited to know the future held his promise safe and it was enough to feel his presence. I left her to indulge. She needed some romance in her single-parent life. Shortly after that, mom died of cancer, and I gave her hippy dresses and books to a salvation army charity shop. We called them junk stores. They were more or less recycle depots for broken dreams. Her New-Age books certainly represented those. Looking back, I can see that efficiency in a time of grief and confusion is a futile coping strategy.

After an hour I felt Jon nudge my arm with his foot and I looked up from my pages into the eyes of a disgruntled man. He held his book up and made a tortured face.

"This stuff is painful," he said. "I don't think I can read much more. I need some coffee to keep me awake. How can women read such romantic drivel?"

"I honestly don't know, I'm a mystery reader."

"Well anyone swallowing *this is* a mystery," he said.

"Maybe you should just take a nap," I said, "there's no need for both of us to suffer. I'm used to reading all day."

"You won't mind?"

"Not one bit, but I can make you coffee if you really want some."

"No. Maybe it's best not to disturb this set-up," he said, shifting Luke to one side. "I can snooze here for a half hour just fine."

"I shall battle on and make you coffee when you wake up," I said.

A little after midnight, Jon staggered, bleary-eyed to the bedroom for some serious sleep while I plowed on skipping through grandiose postulating, flamboyant descriptions, and lurid melodramatic passages of bumpf, racing past overblown archetype villains, and vapid inbred women, reading passages twice for content. The gist was love propaganda, no holds barred. I was learning a lot about Emily's hypersensitive era. Only women starved for intimacy would lean towards such bloated promises of physical love that transported one across past lives. But then, the whole ghosts existing thing had blown my narrow concepts sky-high.

I noticed that none of Marie's rugged heroes sported the ghastly beards of the day. They were always clean-shaven buccaneer-tough alpha males who wore white shirts and lace cravats, their hair tied back with a black ribbon. Dashing good pirates.

I distilled Ms. Corelli's theory as this: after many lifetimes of playing hard to get, staggering betrayals, and violent detours, lovers are destined to meet, but one of the two resists love, leaving the other no other option but to wait out as many lifetimes as it takes for their mate to catch-up. It was bereft of science.

The last incarnation nearest to ultimate consummation was the most frustrating for the spouse-to-be, wasting away on love row. Plots sickened and twisted into Celtic knots of human despair until it was embarrassing to be a member of the Homo Sapien Club. Marie's endings were smarmy throat-constricting heaves of drivel. Pap for the Queen's most ardent copycats. Her female survivors had little recourse but to turn to the entertainments of psychic love, from fortune tellers and Ouija boards to the latest craze for séances and mediums. Promises of love to come had to suffice. Wishing wells and hope chests were for the metaphysically challenged.

The least resistant partner, Marie said, would feel the pull of erotic gravity, and if resolute enough, would become a conduit of magnetic attraction. Powerful stuff, but Darwinian daft, because the weakest link decided the outcome. She went on that: love denied made the bodies containing the souls mentally and physically ill, so as far as *that* went, 'Corelli love' seemed to parallel regular love in that it disrupted commonsense and ethics, and was also a successful appetite suppressant.

Heightened love, Marie expounded, must lure soul mates attuned to a finer frequency, while fear would push them away. Rather a pointless display of ersatz physics, but polarity explained a lot about powder-puff love. Soul mates were doomed to give each other the classic 'hard time'. Both would fight to the death, but one fought for union while the other resisted. Stalemate love prevailed. "Incredibly stale mates," I thought.

It was not a difficult concept to understand it was just ridiculous to accept. But Marie was clever, she proposed a tidy enough illusion to warrant a belief in divine intervention that was sloppy enough to be human. Maybe she *had* been a savvy businesswoman.

For the poor, the desperate, the spurned, the un-beautiful wallflowers, and all others doomed to vicarious love, Marie's explanation was a welcome scenario, but nirvana is an old concept revived for the wistful of every epoch. For us it's the movies and big-screen romance. I call it band-aid love. Marie called it destiny.

The female populace of the Victorian era became hooked on metaphysical bigamy. Married to live spouses yet all the while remaining constant to their ghostly lovers, and I couldn't blame a generation of women sold into wedlock for property rights. To borrow a famous quote: it was the start of something big.

A mere eighty years post-Marie's *Romance of Two Worlds*, the art of 'higher' marriage was intuitively jarred into a mass movement of consciousness which craved a divine answer, and so the 'New-Age' was born to accommodate and exceed all marital expectations. One might even say it was contrived by entrepreneurs. Marie would have been proud to know her books were reborn as a renaissance of her ghostly gentlemen callers.

Cross-dimensional matchmaking eclipsed and explained the disharmony of superficial romantic relationships. The old format was dissipating and it was 'all hail' the new model. It was the time, astronomically speaking, for Aquarius to rule, and his ruling was for the collective of planetary lost couples to pull themselves together. It was akin to a biblical last judgement and thinking of it brought a ghastly image of souls rising from the grave in a bizarre high school reunion as a group migration of soul chemicals aligned to karma. Transitions are tough if not fair.

In other words it was bosh, but all the reading and theories made my brain ramble and in combination with my recently expanded belief system, the Halloween party conjured in my mind was too near the mark of Emily and Martyn's mission. It was time for a crash.

It was safer to resume my cynical teenage attitude that the wallets of the heartbroken and the lonely were gathered into a fold of compassionate bunkum convinced their soul mates were also being drawn by divine providence to the same coordinates for a romantic collision. But, like Marie's promises, soul mate fever delivered an anesthetic of happiness to soothe the victims of rocky romance, so it did *some* good, I suppose.

More personally, Emily's ghost was either proof

of life after death or at least *haunting* after death, or that I was delusional, and that I couldn't sanction.

Jon woke me with a kiss and a cup of tea the next morning. "Gotta go darling one," he said. "I've taken Jen for his morning break, and fed everyone. I don't know how you do it," he said.

"Do what?"

"Read for hours without end every day," he said. "I'll see you tonight."

Emily and Woo knocked on my apartment door at noon, it was the first time I felt respected. Woo darted towards the books on the table weighing down Emily's shoebox and jumped up and down in a frenzy on top of them. I shooed her off, picked one up, and addressed Emily.

"You do realize this is a ridiculous story," I said, waving *The Life Everlasting* in one hand, brandishing it like a politician with a cause.

"And you do realize, you are talking to someone who is reading from that *other side* you're so fond of reminding me about," Emily retorted in a huff.

"Yes," I replied, "I grant that you *do* have a unique perspective."

"It's a telling, remember?" Emily said. "We discussed that. I am telling not suggesting. Not asking. Not discussing. That book you're waving about like a demented preacher, is a guide. I grant you, it's pure syrup, but... and I say *but*... it is nonetheless true. Drop the sentimental slush and it becomes evident.

"Since it's a telling, why couldn't you just tell us," I asked. "Why make us search for it?"

"Science has to be written down and published

to be valid," Emily said. "My opinion would only have been hearsay. It's a damn shame that Miss Corelli's language is so drawn out. I agree with you, it's regrettably saccharine, but I only ask you to act as if it *were* true and suspend your judgement. Can you do that?"

"I can."

"But *will* you?" Emily stressed.

"I will *try*."

"Mercy child! I asked you a serious question. *Will you or not*?"

"I will."

"There's no need to believe it, just give it the benefit of the doubt," she insisted.

Trust Jon to find the embedded gem within the pages that he had glossed over, but it gave us the excuse to stay in for another day of togetherness. I had read too hard. But then I was also the most resistant of the two of us regarding the paranormal despite the arrival of Emily and Regina.

There was a sentence or two in each volume about atoms and electricity, and some mention of radium and references to photosynthesis which made even less sense. I could understand the concept of electricity relating to life, what with Frankenstein and Walt Whitman's 'body electric'. Emily was a fan of Whitman, so, I looked up the *Leaves of Grass* that she was always quoting and read. I could hardly bear to put it down. What I read astounded me. Whitman's words took possession of me. It was the stuff of unbridled desire and worship of the human form. I determined to read him again with more awareness.

I SING THE BODY ELECTRIC
~ Walt Whitman ~
1855

I sing the Body electric;
The armies of those I love engirth me, and I engirth them;
They will not let me off till I go with them, respond to them,
And discorrupt them, and charge them full with the charge
of the Soul. Was it doubted that those who corrupt their own
bodies conceal themselves; and if those who defile the living
are as bad as they who defile the dead?
And if the body does not do as much as the Soul?
And if the body were not the Soul, what is the Soul?

This is the female form;
A divine nimbus exhales from it from head to foot;
It attracts with fierce undeniable attraction!
I am drawn by its breath as if I were no more than a
helpless vapor—all falls aside but myself and it;
Books, art, religion, time, the visible and solid earth,
the atmosphere and the clouds, and what was expected
of heaven or fear'd of hell, are now consumed; mad filaments,
ungovernable shoots play out of it—the response likewise
ungovernable; hair, bosom, hips, bend of legs, negligent falling
hands, all diffused - mine too diffused; ebb stung by the flow,
and flow stung by the ebb, love-flesh swelling and deliciously
aching; limitless limpid jets of love hot and enormous, quivering
jelly of love, white-blow and delirious juice; Bridegroom night
of love, working surely and softly into the prostrate dawn;
Undulating into the willing and yielding day, lost in the cleave
of the clasping and sweet-flesh'd day.

With this volume in her possession, Emily was hardly in need of a Victorian Romance novel. It went on for many more stanzas – heady and more erotic than anything Marie had wrought in her complex plots of hide-and-seek-love.

Ironically, art was Emily's excuse to reject Martyn. As if there wasn't enough love in the eyes of an artist to handle more than one kind of love, and typical, that Martyn, the least resistant of the two, would overstep his approach and try to come to Emily's aid. Unfortunately, stepping up the courtship had the opposite effect, similar to trying to escape from a Chinese finger trap - the more one struggled the more the trap tightened. Trying too hard for anything brought its own disastrous results.

While Martyn was working the extra mile, Emily turned tail and ran, and the further she ran, Martyn compensated and pursued. It's an old story. Young lovers, giddy and mismatched in emotional maturity, grow apart, until in old age there are two lonely hearts separated by miles of regret. Perhaps sacrificed to great works, but discontent and mooning over some thing or someone they can't quite place, waking from dreams too exquisite to bear.

Marie implied that the separated pairs of lovers often met in dreams or as the invisible playmates of childhood. The blindfold was lifted after death. I pitied Martyn. The divine Miss C wrote the book on mule rules, and Emily was never one to waffle over rules. She was sure of the fence and the side she claimed as hers, adamant the other side was less green.

Point for point, Emily was a classic Corelli heroine, aggressively trained, dedicated and thwarted to bitterness. Softening over time was unknown. Time rendered Emily opinionated with defenses overblown to disguise a crushed spirit. So far, Emily was a Corelli femme fatale to a T.

Then I thought of Woo. Perhaps it was she who was Emily's soul mate. They loved and fought and argued as a duet, an angst-driven inseparable pair that had become a single iconic entity. The old dear with a monkey growing out of her shoulder. Two irascible creatures with a mind to controlling any room they were in.

I reported back. Emily was impatient. "Well, what did you learn?"

"*The Leaves of Grass* is one wild book, and I think you and Woo are soul mates," I said, waiting for the verbal blows to fall.

"Of course she isn't," Emily scoffed. "Woo is my guardian angel."

"Emily!"

"Scottie!"

"Woo is a monkey! Are you insane?"

"Love makes people say crazy things," she said.

"No," I replied. "Love makes people *do* crazy things."

The world is horrid
right straight through, and so am I.
I am a pail of milk that has gone sour.

~ Emily Carr ~
Hundreds and Thousands

Whereabouts Known

walked briskly towards home where Jon waited with a bear hug, slippers, and tea – a natural wonder of unselfish tenderness. Mine all mine. What did I care for ghosts and art that goes bump in the night?

Jon cared. Which meant I remained open and eager to please him, and by doing so, would reap some financial benefits for our future, as well as please Emily Carr and her *spirited* Java monkey. We were some team.

I passed the corner of Government Street, taking the scenic route behind the looming bulk of the Empress Hotel. I saw the peripheral silhouette of a baby carriage pushed by a hunched mother who, when confronted, disappeared into wheezy laughter and cigar smoke.

"Tease!" I shouted into the scent of stale tobacco, and startled the man approaching who was walking a skittish terrier. They had been on a collision course with an apparition. I reined in Jenner for my own peace of mind. Napoleon syndrome may be a human myth, but short canines won't be gainsaid. Large dogs drive little dogs berksic.

The man nodded politely as his snappy dog bared its teeth, snarling like a demon. He felt nothing untoward from his pet, numb to the destruction it likely wreaked every day, but I saw him shiver as he crossed the threshold of Emily's dissipating energy.

It was unnerving to realize that Emily had become more like my stalker.

Marie

For the explicit reason that Marie's books were a Victorian froth of estrogen and false hope, I googled her and read her online stats. What Emily would call her 'biog'. She was born Mary Mackay, but unsatisfied with its cachet, when she decided to go public she appropriated a more flamboyant name from a travelling musician. So, she wasn't savvy in a formal way, she was just plain calculating. As I read on, I realized Marie Corelli had not only been eccentric; she was basically certifiable.

The Romance of Two Worlds was first published in 1886, and no doubt the first copy headed towards Balmoral and Her Majesty.

Queen Victoria, was the consummate two-faced morality goddess, who feverishly followed any notion which claimed that love conquered death. Any theory which fanned the notion of meeting Prince Albert again was eagerly accepted without question. In my opinion she was equally keen to dish out rules of abstinence and frigidity to all others, but then she sanctioned the paranormal, so she wasn't all that stuffy.

Emily had likely missed this book's debut (being ten at the time) and under the jurisdiction of a Lizzie, hell-bent on traveling first-class to heaven – the pious sister, who would never have dreamed of admitting to housing such dreadful tomes under her regime. Mental sex was dizzifying enough. Dizzy Lizzy could read accordingly and take smelling salts, and remain 'intacta', but a precocious girl of ten who could snoop and read, may have infiltrated her big sister's cache of contraband. I made a note to ask Emily.

From Emily's anecdotes, Lizzie would hardly have read novels of an erotic nature unless they'd been placed into her hands in the privacy of her own boudoir. But Miss Lizzie Carr *was* human, ergo, I expect a lot of hush-hush unraveled in there, to be tightly-corseted in the light of day. My theory was that guilt mixed with jealousy made Lizzie more stern with Emily and possibly made her a tad sexually frustrated in her chosen position as the family iceberg.

Emily confirmed my suspicions: "It wasn't me who gave Lizzie those books, it was Clara. I found them a few years after and shared them with Alice. I understood the dynamics of celibacy and passion very well. I told you I was an accomplished tease." Five sisters allowed for a plethora of book exchange opportunities.

The later title, *The Life Everlasting*, was released in 1911. Queen Victoria missed that one by ten years, but by then, Emily was a resolute near-heathen, and well-read in open view of the ruckus she generated. Emily was an independent forty-year-old who welcomed sisters Lizzie and Alice's wrath at every opportunity.

I re-read the blurb on the forty year-old paperback's weathered sixteenth edition. The back cover read:

> *...a strange love story of both mortal and immortal passion, combined with some startling suggestions on the actual causes of life and death... ...a daring and original work which should bring hope and consolation to many for whom the present life seems futile and the future uncertain.*

No wonder it had hooked my desperate mother.

The prologue was a whopping thirty-three page cloyingly-apologetic effort, meant to bolster the reader's confidence that the eventual written words to follow were the scientific duty of a responsible reporter rather than a quick melodramatic thrill for virgins. It had been in this section where Jon found the references to science.

Given the overall theme of lovers meeting unsuccessfully over several lifetimes, it was fair to assume that Emily feared a few karmic blots against her name, demanding, as she was, perfect alignment over a journey of broken dreams while Martyn rested.

I knew the why and who of Emily's quest from the start; now I knew what she was working with.

She had regained her insight after death and was ready to accept that her retrograde friendship with Martyn had been the act of a semi-conscious woman with an ability to thwart her deep emotions and override her soul. Emily was certainly capable of thinking *that*. Now, she wanted to be exonerated at all costs.

Theirs' had been a shipboard romance between two kindred fears on the road to recognition. One yielding and waiting; the other resistant upholding the laws and the Queen's honour.

Martyn worked on board the *Willapa* and needed the open sea, which is why, after Emily, he abandoned it for California as penance, and became a real estate entrepreneur inland. My Jon, is similarly cleaved to the ocean, but comfortable everywhere. I was a mermaid with sea sickness on any form of float. Land and sea, earth and water, all of us were receptive or hardened to the realities of romance.

If anyone could be the parallel of Emily's eccentricity, it was Marie Corelli. Marie spoke fake Italian for effect; lived in a house in Stratford-on-Avon that had once belonged to Shakespeare's sister; and kept a gondola tethered to her river landing at the bottom of her garden. She also kept a mistress and alienated her neighbors.

Emily just had Woo.

I have loved three souls passionately.
I have known friendship, jealousy,
and dreadful hurt.

~ Emily Carr ~
The Shadow of War
1938

Love During
the Time of Woo Woo

or two days I avoided Beacon Hill
Park and Emily's wishes faded
naturally into the background of
my life. Apparently the living had some rights. Jon
told me that the deceased who were unhappy and
connected to unfinished business, fed on the sadness and fear of the living, not because they were
ghouls, but because their energies matched. People
who feared ghosts were more likely to have a fright-
ful confrontation or feel a restless spirit.

Since graveyards make humans anxious they
were by definition, a hotspot for sightings. "Emotions have an organic nature that generates energy.
An open mind is receptive," he had said. There
were very few cheerful spectres because happy in-
dividuals had usually moved on.

Much later, Jon and I came to understand that
strong emotions of joy tuned Emily and Woo out, or
to be more accurate, confused the wavelength of our
communication. But I had noticed, that whenever

I was daydreaming or tired, I was frequented by Emily's visitations.

My thoughts had been concentrated on Jon. I hadn't been dismissive on purpose. Jenner and I were headed to Jon's apartment after our shortcut through Saint Ann's, and as we approached the museum, I glanced to my right from the corner of Belleville and Government – the corner where Emily's statue loomed, larger than life, yet smaller than soul. Jenner whined an alert.

I saw the bronze Woo move and dissolve into bright colors. She inclined her head towards my energy. I was in for it. I had been joking that morning to Jon about the cold and its reference to 'brass monkeys'. Probably that tipped off Woo.

It was chilly. For a moment my thoughts had been unguarded, focused on my physical reaction to the weather. Its effect on my exposed neck had broken my magic mood and I adjusted my wool scarf. Wind off the harbour could be surprisingly brisk any day of the year. My earlier brass monkey remark came to mind which led to an image of Woo's statue. Perhaps that was all that was necessary to send Woo the signal that gave me away.

Woo had entered the statue, taking her position on Emily's bronze shoulder, scanning the evening activity. Her pink face lit up seeing me. She did her victory dance. I was caught in her headlights.

"Hi," I sent to her, "What can I do for you mi-lady?"

"Plenty," answered Emily's raspy old voice from behind me.

Emily appeared from the shadows. She turned towards me and vanished in a puff of bitter smoke.

Woo Woo   VERONICA KNOX

A smoldering old stogy remained steaming on the pavement. Like I needed a reminder. She was in a foul mood.

"Okay," I shouted towards the oily darkness of the harbour: "I hear you."

A passerby gave me a wide berth.

"We need to be on the same page," admonished Emily's disembodied voice. "The same map, the same calendar, the same mission. You can swoon on your own time."

"I thought I was," I argued, mentally.

"In your whole library, haven't you read any of those pact-with-the-devil stories? You sold your soul to me for a few days. Not much to ask if you want to keep those letters."

"Rented, not sold," I corrected. "Does that make you the devil?"

Woo's answer was a devilish yowl which failed to reassure me. "Borrowed," I yelled out loud. I lowered my voice to regular speaking volume, and added: "Possibly hi-jacked. Never sold."

Emily's resounding laugh reminded me of a stereotypical pirate listening to a parlay they've no intention of honoring, and I spoke with more restraint."I *may* have compromised my soul for a few days in a mad moment. Please allow me some reflections of sanity."

"Love is not sanity missy, but it *is* a form of blindness. I'm still in the throes of it, so I should know. It's called a heightened state of awareness for a reason, but you,"... she wheezed, proud of herself, "you are besotted. You just crossed the road without looking and narrowly missed a permanent bunk in Ross Bay 'Gardens'."

"Sorry Mum," I said, and continued my journey, heads up, staring ahead into my future with Jon.

"Look Dearie," came the soft voice close to my left ear. "I want to leave tomorrow. Early."

"Dearie? Who are you now? A witch peddling a poison apple? No wait, I forgot. You're my fairy godmother?"

"I don't give a damn who I appear to be," Emily retorted huffily. "It's time we were away. Please pick me up outside Saint Joseph's Apartments at 5 am, tomorrow. You can breakfast on your delectable drive-through fare on the road."

I spluttered with laughter. "You are too much."

Emily's mercurial temper softened once more, "Well, of course I'm too much. I come with a monkey," she replied, and I felt my old pal, Miss Emily Carr-that-was, nudge my shoulder in fun. She had said, please.

I understand privacy. I also understand contracts. My task, simply restated, was to locate the burial site of William Mayo Paddon, take Emily there, wait for contact with the aforementioned Martyn, act as pre-nup marriage counsellor, and lead them back to the cemetery time forgot. Straightforward and simple.

Emily and I had prearranged for Jon to ride shotgun, but when he first volunteered Woo had flown into a rage of protest and scampered off like a small mad windmill.

The four of us would find Martyn together. No way, would Emily fly. I would have bet that the deceased were over their fear of crashing to earth in flames, but I failed to reckon on my own superstition and Emily's need for time on the road to prepare. I also had no idea of the curvaceous hardball heading my way.

I hurried to Jon's apartment to leave a note. We had packing to do. I searched for a pen and paper on his desk where a red light flashed merrily. The recorded message on Jon's answer machine was soft and clear, as Trudi intended:

Beeeeep: *"Hi sweetie, it's me. Sorry I had to cancel before. I'm calling for a rain-check. Wondering if your cousin has gone on her little trip yet? Can't wait to see you in our old place... kiss kiss."* Beeeeep.

I was incensed. "My *little* trip?" I shrieked into my phone. I could imagine Jon holding his receiver several inches from his ear. He said what all men everywhere say in such a situation: "I can explain if you just calm down."

What do you suppose Lord Sebastian wanted?
A hairbrush for his teddy-bear...
... he bought a very nice one with an ivory back
and he's having Aloysius engraved on it
– that's the bear's name.

~ Evelyn Waugh ~
Brideshead Revisited
1945

A Journey Begins
with the Last Step

*J*on had left a red rose and the antique teddy-bear we had found during our first days together, on my passenger seat. The toy with the bandaged torn ear that wasn't for sale. He had no doubt finessed it with his charm. It had a yellow ribbon around its neck, and the florist's card tucked into the bandage read: *Beware of seagulls bear-ing gifts. It means they love you. Sorry I can't be with you. I was keeping Aloysius for our first anniversary, but this occasion takes the cake. Have a safe trip. Love Sebastian a.k.a Jon Living Stone Seagull.*

The 'other matter' had been shelved in a pique of hastily resolved feelings, after Emily had announced Jon had to stay home. She gave her reason as a conflict of interest, explaining the discord between him and I would distort the positive energy she wanted to generate. Hardly the way to begin a trip, but it made sense.

Emily was there as promised. Sitting on the edge of a wrought-iron chair at the top of the cement steps to my apartment. No sign of Woo. I raised my eyebrows in a silent question of where? Emily whistled through her fingers. A bright yellow dot moved in the trees across the street like a giant canary, swooped over the street and surprisingly landed on *my* shoulder.

"Morning sunshine," I said to Woo, noting the overcast sky and Woo's present colour. I felt a sharp nip on my ear as tiny princess hands fondled the hoop earring in my left ear and tugged gently to test its resistance. I didn't wait for the next move. I took it off and handed it to Woo as a bribe. She eyed the other one with obvious longing and got that one too.

As I buckled up, Woo spied Marmie on the dashboard where I had posed her beside the rose, holding Jon's note. I grabbed the card seconds before monkey hands whisked Marmie away. I met Emily's eyes. "I guess you don't have to use your seatbelt," I said, and turned the ignition.

It was beginning to sprinkle when my silver Cavalier swung left off Humboldt, leaving behind its gracious shady lanes for the concrete tunnel of central downtown and the dawn rush hour of Douglas Street. We would make our ferry with time to spare.

My passengers were eager. Woo showed off by acting like an electron bouncing from one side of the car to the other as rain peppered the windshield in a comforting benediction. I kept my sunglasses handy for eye-strain and to disguise the occasional tearing up. Jon separation and the 'kindness of bear' eclipsed my anger and I felt emotionally ripped in half. I recovered and let Woo's antics refocus my attention.

"She's going to stir herself into a crazy thing," I said, meaning *more* crazy.

Emily shook her head. "Actually, she's weaving. This is one of her calming rituals. She must be centered for this trip."

"Well, she looks like she's going to hurt herself."

"Woo is gathering energy, so she will be a compass for us."

It almost made sense. Energy is invisibly located and atmospheric.

Emily explained: "Woo has to prepare herself. She responds to a subtle form of magnetism."

"So, she has to wind herself up like a clockwork toy to make some sort of contact with her inner power?" I suggested.

"You see. I knew you would understand."

"Woo is too high-strung," I said. "She's behaving like a Tasmanian Devil. She should meditate if she wants to get centered, especially if she's a sensitive homing device."

"When Woo is agitated, her movements are accompanied by shrieks. Do you hear any shrieking?"

I hadn't noticed how quiet Woo was in her leapings and twirlings. "Not a peep," I agreed. Woo's silent antics made her expression eerie. Her wild eyes flashed with human intelligence and she gnashed her jaws like a creature gasping for breath. Finally, she stopped and stole my rose off the dashboard, cupped the head of it into her hands and plucked it from its stem. It looked like she was holding a small red apple.

Woo buried her nose into the red petals and took a first bite. She scattered the rest over Emily's head. Then she took the stem and began waving it about like a wand, first innocently and then tapping me harder and harder about the shoulders. All the while she chewed and chattered a monkey mantra with her eyes closed in ecstasy.

I grabbed the rose stem from Woo, rolled down the window, and sent it winging. Woo watched it disappear into the rain and sent me a look of bewilderment. I almost felt sorry for her, but it had been dangerous. The wand had been poked perilously close to my eye.

I received the full brunt of a spoiled child's tantrum for my audacity and Woo's expression returned to her mesmerizing stare.

I remembered what Emily had said about Woo being in control. She had said it like a warning. Was this jungle imp controlling my will? I dared not look into those crazed eyes.

Emily nodded haughtily after reading my mind, "Meditate on *that*," she said, with a smile of triumph.

I left a hasty message on Jon's phone. "Hey Seagull. Thank you for Aloysius. I love him. He makes me feel safe. Call me. It feels as if you are with me, after all. Call me okay? Lots of bear hugs. Don't forget to call me." I had said *call me* three times in ten seconds. I shook my brain and paid attention to the road. A wave of dizziness passed over me and I opened the window to gulp down some air. The rain sprinkled my face and revived me. Woo was opening and closing the glove compartment and shredding the paper napkins stored there. I thought of Bette Davis' famous line in 'All About Eve' – this was going to be a bumpy ride, except maybe not; I was wearing my lucky sweater.

Emily soon hunched herself into a position of isolation, leaning her forehead on the passenger window, deep in thought. Woo abandoned Marmie for Aloysius, larger than herself, and sat peering into his button eyes for signs of animation.

I suddenly felt the urge to be sick. Nerves, I thought. I sipped bottled water and took deep breaths. I needed to compose myself before I spoke with Jon, so when my phone buzzed like a dying bee and vibrated feebly on the dashboard, I ignored it, playing hard to get.

Woo gave up on the bear and returned to Marmie. I made a mental note to call Jon when I had regained my equilibrium and to retrieve my earrings at the next opportunity. Marmie was determined to keep hers, but Woo wiggled it frantically like a loose tooth.

I received one letter from Sebastian...
... it was written on, and enveloped in,
heavy late-Victorian mourning paper,
black-coroneted and black-bordered.
I read it eagerly ...
... I have a good mind not to take Aloysius to Venice.
I don't want him to meet a lot of disagreeable Italian bears
and pick up bad habits.

~ Evelyn Waugh ~
Brideshead Revisited
1945

Driving Miss Emily

A girl monkey wearing a lemon-yellow dress, sporting a pair of gold bangle bracelets stared into the downpour, and made misty patches of monkey breath on the glass. I half expected Woo to trace a happy face with her finger.

I planned to make a deal with Woo, later – an exchange of a kipper for my best earrings.

My little navigator wanted to direct traffic, but had to settle for giving the driver beside us a dressing down when he sped through the lights and cut us off. "Maybe I should get myself a monkey," I thought. "A sidekick who can express the things I want to say but can't."

"Praps' not," Emily butted in. "Monks are not for the faint of heart."

"I consider my heart healthier than yours, Madame," I said.

"I was speaking of romance," Emily said, sarcastically.

"So was I."

Woo turned herself pale champagne yellow to match the faded bear. Her dress was white cotton to match the bandage. She raked the dog blanket in the back seat into a nest and cuddled little Marmie, chirruping words of comfort as she examined the stump of her missing tail. In my rear-view mirror I watched Woo continue to worry the distinctive brass manufacturer's tag in Marmie's ear. I informed Emily that the miniature plaque was a sign of authenticity and that removing it, devalued it. "Leave that blessed thing be!" Emily shrieked at Woo.

Driving gave me a degree of normalcy. I was relieved to be speaking aloud again. The rain came stronger now as a curtain between our transport pod and the eyes in the cars either side of us. Emily, looked very smart in the passenger seat, opaque as you please, dressed in a dark-blue serge traveling suit, buttoned up high at the neck, the bit of lace at her throat was adorned with an Art Deco tie pin encrusted with garnets. She wore short white kid gloves.

For the duration of the trip, I assumed Emily would remain her twenty-seven year-old self. The age she had been when she met Martyn, William Mayo Paddon, aboard the steamer, *Willapa*.

I shoulder-checked to change lanes and sneaked

a peek at Emily. Surprisingly, she looked slightly flushed as any young woman would, thinking about her beau with expectations beyond ordinary enduring. Her gloved hands picked nervously at the buttons on her jacket and she fanned herself with the folded roadmap. Every now and then she glanced at the scenery and sighed.

My cell phone lay far too quietly on the dashboard. Watching it wouldn't make it burst into song any faster. I wanted it to ring so I could ignore it again and wasn't sure why. It behaved in the same brooding manner as its landline brothers, in a bubble of excruciating silence when charged with waiting for a lover's return call. It seemed all the more ominous, as it had rarely stopped ringing from Jon's attention since the day we met. It seemed to sulk. Being reduced to the slavery of a business trip; it had become a cold little rectangle of ominous silver plastic.

It was only right that Emily had dissuaded Jon from coming the night he and I had the row over Trudi. Her rendezvous with Martyn was at stake. I had been recruited to realize it, not jeopardize it. Emily convinced Jon that our vibes would compromise the mission. He and I were tense and who was I to question the rules of a woman almost seventy years dead? Miss *Millie* called the shots, assisted by her 'familiar' although I was beginning to think it may be the other way around.

Jon was resigned to waiting for my reports. If he was mad at me or Emily, there was nothing I could do about it. I tried to think happy thoughts. I had some priceless letters which would enable me to buy a house with a garden for Jenner, and bankroll Jon's book about paranormal contact. We had a rosy chance, but I felt queasy thinking about it.

Trudi was a beautiful woman with predator instincts. It wasn't Jon's fault she prowled after the trail of musk he exuded. I couldn't blame her for that, but her message had hinted of a postponed tête a tète. Jon had never mentioned arranging such a thing, but Trudi's words implied he had.

Emily smiled over at me, "Scottie what will be will be," she said.

I missed Jon's third call when I paid for gas inside the service station. I tried to return it, but the lack of bars on my phone told me a recharge was required. I remained unsettled, squirming in my car seat waiting the designated hour for a strong signal.

No man had called me darling before. It was very English, and surprisingly, from Jon's Canadian lips it sounded natural. I had tried saying it back once and it tangled my tongue. Romantic endearment was not a language I used with ease. Honey, Hon, Sweetheart, Sweetie, Baby and Babe, were names American's used trippingly, but they rang too false for me. I had dubbed Jon, Sebastian or Seagull for a reason – in casual homages to our 'Brideshead' riff and, more obviously, 'Jonathan Livingston'. They were less intimate, but I used them with undisguised affection. I wanted to protect myself from sounding too eager.

We drove in and out of various stages of rain, and passed a dog walker with a bouquet of dogs trying to shift her umbrella into a functioning position. Emily turned to watch, her expression wistful.

"We made a different kind of splash, my menagerie and I," she commented. "We kept Victorians on their toes. I heard their tsk tsks. I saw them look away embarrassed to know me.

The more shock appeal the better, I say. It was my way of standing on a soapbox. I detested the few who smiled indulgently, as if I was a mental case to be pitied. Sometimes I swore at them on purpose to get a negative reaction, but they moved off, hoping to restore their sense of propriety."

"Maybe once in a while they deserved the Sunday-best Emily," I suggested.

"I never smoked on the street, but they saw me and my cigar at an open window many a time. I waved it at them in case they missed the effect. Friendly smiles turned to horror as they picked up their pace and manoeuvred their children into huddles of 'don't ask so many questions dear' – but the little ones didn't care. They wanted to see the monk and knew I always carried a decent selection of boiled sweets in my pocket."

We plowed slowly through the downfall as lightning streaking from our destination, and finally left the rain's wrath on the highway. We took an off-ramp that led into to a soft mist. Very surreal. We could hear the muted sting of thunder. Woo was white as a traditional ghost, asleep on Emily's knee. Emily leaned forward eagerly when she saw the ferry. Woo looked dead, but when I braked at the ticket booth she stirred slightly and started to snore.

The ferry's cafeteria was the usual bustle. I joined the queue for clam chowder and coffee that smelled more appetizing in the salty air. I was ravenous. I allowed myself to be. I was pursued by a man who thought me perfect and I was inside an adventure. I felt excited. I had a lovely man to come home to, and did I mention he called me darling?

Restaurant etiquette should stipulate that no monkeys are allowed behind the counter, but Woo peered under each metal lid of the entree dishes as they were opened and stole a taste. When she was done with hot food, she found the cutlery and condiment counter and began selecting pouches and small containers of butter and coffee cream. These she collected in a heap beside Emily. She clambered onto our table and ripped open her assortment of foil pouches and paper lids, retreating for more when she was satisfied the contents had been dumped, tossed, scattered or sampled.

Woo sneezed from inhaling too deeply into a paper packet marked pepper and shrieked her disgust at the smell of mustard. Emily told Woo to desist, and for a moment I thought she might, but she swung away from us to explore an elderly woman's open purse, who sat near us.

Emily had a sporadic attitude to real-time food which made her the perfect dining companion. She could rattle on and I didn't have to respond. She was an audio book, and her ethereal state enabled her words to enter my mind like headphones.

I was happy to listen to her talk and gave my attention to the savoury soup in front of me. Today it was the Manhattan variety. I was content. The buzz of milling passengers reduced my bizarre mission to an ordinary excursion and I welcomed their life signs. I dreaded going back to the car.

Emily had a lot to remember and therefore to impart. I was beginning to think of her as Millie as she fidgeted with her gloves and smiled into the past. I waved her to continue speaking with my soup spoon as my mouth was full.

"Martyn and I, we had that twin thing," Emily volunteered, "I didn't know it at the time. Neither of us were fully aware of our connection, and we were rarely together long enough to compare notes, so it was relatively subtle.

In 1906, I was back home living under my sister's house rules, and I had a 'turn'. What we called an episode of indeterminate mental confusion."

"You mean the a dizzy spell?" I offered, between mouthfuls.

"More like fainting from emotional stimulation," she said.

"Pray tell," I said.

"I had been in a sound sleep," Emily began, "when I heard my name being called with alarming intensity: 'Millie! Millie! Where are you?'

I woke to bedlam. Chilled without my eiderdown and blankets, which I had kicked to the floor. This was odd, because it was nippy for mid-April.

My eyes were open. I could sense a familiar room, but the dream persisted in a landscape I did not recognize. It was vivid. There had been a battle. The aftermath of war was spread flat as if I looked down on it from a hill. I saw heaps of crumbled bricks and smouldering rubble from a bomb disaster. It was like the newspaper's war photos from the front. A demilitarized zone of unspeakable destruction.

I experienced remnants of the dream all day: I had been searching a field hospital for my brother, and then remembered that Dick had been dead for seven years. Still the feeling of concern for a loved one persisted.

Fire licked the edges of my furnishings which appeared slowly out of the darkness. Toppled books were spread in a swathe over the small flowered carpet, dresser drawers were pulled out, and a heap of clothes were strewn across the floor. I shivered and found my slippers on opposite sides of the room. From the streets, came sounds of terrified horses, people screaming, and sirens, and the acrid smell of smoke.

The house felt normal, but I crept downstairs and opened the door. The street was deserted and I felt reassured, so I made myself a cup of strong milky tea with three heaping spoonfuls of sugar. The clock had stopped on twelve-past-five.

I invoked the name Billy to center myself, and sent him my usual: *hello it's me again* thought. I sent these mental telegraphs from time to time when I had my worse panic attacks. I said his name whenever I needed to feel safe. Billy would protect me. I felt that. I relied on it. In a crisis, he was there, always out of sight, patient, always waiting hat-in-hand for a kind word of encouragement from me. His name held power for me. He was my medicine. My first defense.

My thoughts were visited by a collage of 'Billy snapshots', each polished square clung to a black page by silver corner stickers, our courtship flashed before me in pictures. I saw him gazing with adoration, walking towards me, grinning, arms wide,

WooWoo VERONICA KNOX

then looking at me from over the top of his newspaper, or holding open a door, or the gallant with a posy of violets, then in windy profile leaning on the deck of the *Willapa*, I saw him opening our garden gate, and on horseback, and rocking on the veranda of Carr House. The images sped up and unwound into a flickering stream, appearing like an early film. They finally resumed the look of a newsreel documentary where people in the streets walked like dazed puppets. Some were crying and wandering disoriented; others looted the gaping holes that were once storefronts.

I couldn't shake the smell of smoke and gas, nor the face I missed so keenly during my odd spells of terror. My big brotherly beau, who wanted to give me his name and take me home as his wife. Despite my aversion to marriage when he stifled me so, I felt a confusion of love.

In a way Martyn, my Billy, *was* family. He moved in on me and was at home with us, sitting in as patriarch at the head of our table. My sister Dede expected my acceptance of an imminent proposal and had been livid to learn how often I refused him. She had no idea. Lizzie smoldered from jealousy.

The smelling salts that I always kept close by, failed to cleanse my nostrils of smoke, but the screams had faded into a Vancouver Island dawn, damp and foggy.

The whistle of the kettle soothed me, which was odd because I loathed the shriek it made, but it was a comfort to be pouring hot water and to inhale the aroma of a waking teapot. I let the heady 'Builder's Tea' steep for longer than usual and tried to spread a scone with cold butter. The butter was so cold, it tore the flesh of the pastry. I glued it back together with orange marmalade. I welcomed the cutting smell of citrus, and the breakfast clatter. I made bread and butter 'soldiers' and a boiled egg that had its own cheerful cosy, like the teapot. Their crocheted coats transported me back to childhood security. I have always loved the simple rituals of breakfast.

The English and their traditions surrounding tea had infiltrated my routine. Tea was my second defense for panic attacks, the triage of nightmares. A strong heavily-sweetened *cuppa* was known to neutralize shocks of all sorts.

I cradled my cup in its saucer, such a small sound, but it defused the horrific images of war and death. I moved to clear the dishes and accidentally dropped a fresh egg on the floor. I saw it fall in slow motion like the last egg of the world. It cracked in two clean halves, and the golden yolk spilled out and burst. I could see a red speck of blood floating in a pool of yellow. I felt ill and fear returned.

But for once, it was not *my* fear, it was Martyn's, so I mentally shared my tea with him and he seemed to rally. The rest of the day told me why I was so alarmed. San Francisco had been levelled by an earthquake and was burning. Somewhere in the chaos was Martyn, alive or dying and in need of me. He had called to me for help and all I could do was make tea.

Marmalade unnerved me after that, but sometimes I ate it to bring Martyn closer. The Christmas mandarins were aligned to his annual greeting card with its pressed flower – a dehydrated blossom which ironically represented our dried-flat relationship. Other times I avoided Marmalade as it made me lonelier than was healthy.

The past is an intrusion. Especially my reveries connected to forest paintings. I was vulnerable to impulsive thoughts that overlapped. Nature and love all brambly and wild. Thorns that tore at my mind daring to rest in some glade of retreat. At those times I was open to my muse. The mythological Green Man, my spouse of choice, had Martyn's face – a heartbroken emperor wearing a crown of laurel. His eyes were stern with me and achingly sad, but it had been I who made the thumbs down motion that condemned our love to death.

There had been so many proposals: on park benches, once in a dark cinema, the top of a double-decker bus, the monkey house at London Zoo, and many many over cups of tea and scones with marmalade. Martyn was always as close as a spoonful of marmalade, the scent of tangerines, or a singing kettle."

I felt the need to check in with Jon and flipped opened my cell phone. Nothing. A passerby saw my frustration and told me I wouldn't get a signal again till we docked. I had forgotten that inconvenience.

I stood up to take my dirty dishes to the tray drop off and felt so woozy I had to clutch the handrail to regain my balance. A vision of buildings toppling in slow motion made me feel claustrophobic and I wanted off the boat for my own equilibrium as much as the ability to call Jon.

I returned to my seat with my stomach churning and put my head on the table, fearful of creating a worse scene.

My own research had encountered the 'jolt through the earth' of the 1906 San Francisco earthquake, known as the Great Fire. I had written in my notes that the force of the split had sent the Salinas River raging six miles off its original course, to Marina, in Monterey County – a significant fact which was now causing sufficient aftershocks of indigestion in my stomach.

"What's the matter?" Emily asked. "You've gone quite pale."

"Bad clams I think. I'll be okay in a minute. I just need some water."

"Maybe you're seasick?"

"I forgot about that. Either way, I feel nauseous."

My solar plexus – the epicenter of my intuition, fluttered with fear. I was starting to remember Emily's life as if it were a series of watercolor paintings; I was a woman under pressure with my own fragile fault line.

I sensed the conjoined coastlines as they must have shuddered, twisting into new valleys and chasms. I was fixated on the lack of stability, more than usual.

After that first day on the road, I had begun to think like my companion. Emily's old excuses and fears crept into my happiness and left a stain that tainted my love for Jon.

I felt my independence slipping from me and finally pulled out of me like the innocent loose thread in an old sweater that one assumes is short but unravels forever. I felt my confidence begin to crumble, and let the next two calls from Jon, ring unanswered, then I packed my lucky sweater at the bottom of my suitcase and wore a new green and khaki camouflage tee shirt. It was an appropriate choice as war seemed to lurk around every corner.

We had planned a coastal route down through Washington and Oregon eventually heading towards San Francisco, hopefully shadowing the landmarks Emily remembered.

San Diego was where Martyn lay buried. The second day we pushed on and I begged Emily to tell me more stories about her life. I told her I needed to stay awake, which was not a lie, but it was more of a distraction to counter a moping spirit, whose presence was having an adverse affect on my own relationship. Doubts crept in where sunshine had made things right. That she-wolf, Trudi, slunk the boundaries of Jon and I. I had left him unattended, and I began to wonder if that wasn't part of Emily's plan. My head hurt from serial headaches and I had to rest, often. My 'battle fatigues' became pyjamas. I was too tired to change my clothes and even slept in my shoes.

I made a mental note that ghosts never stop talking, even if you pull over to the side of the road and snooze yourself. They stay alert, inside your head with a running dialogue of rerun life. Along with secrets, they spill sour milk and vinegar. Apparently, hindsight is power. They don't stop for responses. It's the colourful replay of that life-passing-in-front-of-one's-eyes, with more candid commentary than life's little spontaneous recalls.

Incoming text from Jon shrilled its arrival and I read: *Love means always having to say you're sorry.* Cute. But I felt hardened to cute and wasn't sure why.

The truth was, it was 2012, I was eating a stash of Nanaimo Bars beside Emily Carr, speeding down the highway towards Portland with San Diego an impossibly far off destination on the distant horizon, listening to Pink Floyd, with a ghost monkey exploring the contents of my overnight bag.

"I like this music," Emily said.

"You should," I said, "it's *The Dark Side of the Moon*."

I was on my way to exhume a dead bridegroom – up to my ass in ectoplasm. It was definitely the dark side of somewhere.

It was one of Martyn's asking days;
they always depressed us.

~ Emily Carr ~
Growing Pains

Emily's Blog

had done a double-take the first time I saw an archive photo of Emily's nineteenth century, 5-cent scribbler. Its heading read: Emily's 'BIOG', but the more I looked, the more I substituted a lowercase 'l' for her capital 'I'. To me it read, BLOG.

It's natural for a word-hound's eyes to play snap and connect with a symbol the brain knows. Since I had never referred to a biography with the abbreviation 'biog', I couldn't help *but* see the word blog. In all innocence it was a creative jump for me to make, but Jon was thrilled. He called it a subconscious premonition. He enthused about his 'one missing letter theory' that he's so obsessed with, delighted that another coyote trickster of the English language had behaved in a deviant manner and jumped into his collection.

I told Emily she was either a genius or another psychic, 'Little Miss Nostradamus', like Woo. She declared it was a lucky coincidence. I settled on uncanny.

Jon continued to play subliminal word association with my reference to Emily's insight, especially when

I referred to Emily's chapter headings as 'posts'. I told him: "If Emily blogs, she can post as well," which led to a bit of nonsense about Emily Post, (born only one year after our Emily) who wrote the book on etiquette that stifled a generation of chameleon women from feeling empowered. Language and historic links abound and continue to astound me.

Emily's memoirs are a fever-dream of incidents jumbled together like unwanted items on a yard sale table and the miles went by faster when I let her tell them. Her stories had been suppressed by the confines of the Gilded-Age. Jon had added a letter 'c' and announced that Emily had lived in a gilded *cage*. Emily agreed, and said it was why she was drawn to birds. They were both impossible sometimes.

I had speculated with Jon earlier, why Emily had been drawn to a monkey.

"You could have asked her yourself," he said.

"When monkeys fly," I answered.

Jon reminded me of the flying monkeys from *The Wizard of Oz* and we both agreed: Emily was Auntie Em some days and the wicked witch of the west on others. I was a freaked-out Dorothy, Jenner was Toto, and Woo was definitely Emily's puppeteer, Oz.

Emily settled in for a long confession in a tale that had the affect of adrenalin on my failing energy, because as usual, she was forthright to a fault.

"Lust flabbergasted me," she started out, "and marriage equalled childbirth, not the pleasant companionship of a handsome beau, but the fatal illness of pregnancy, remorse, and grief. I witnessed too many infant deaths. Our family had three brothers reduced to empty names and dates scrawled on the inside cover of our Bible. The endpapers of events: marriages, births, and deaths. Serial motherhood sapped wives of their freedom. Women's bodies and energies stretched threadbare over years of domestic servitude under the auspices of a master patriarch with bigger dreams. Not the little stillbirth frettings we girls were allowed to have.

Human stories always end in a bed of eternal sleep don't they? We live in a parade of beds: conceiving beds, lying-in beds, hospital sickbeds, deathbeds and cold cradles, even lying on satin curtains in a wooden box."

Emily's elderly face grew dark. It aged into a crumpled walnut of remorse. She looked more like Woo's mom than ever. "Oh, I know I shouldn't have sent him away," she confessed. "I knew it at the time. Blasted pride! The words flew out of my mouth and slapped his face before I knew it. Martyn's expression haunts me still, which is my just desserts as I am dead and so is he."

"Clean slate time, Emily. If anyone can convince a corpse to get married, it's you," I said.

Emily stayed silent, but Woo jumped up and down and gave me a loud tongue lashing. "Way to be nice with my earrings on your scrawny little wrists," I said to Woo. I can take those back right now."

I grabbed for Woo's arm and missed. She ran to Emily to escape my reach.

"You've been told!" Emily said, calming Woo with a hug.

Emily gave me a look over her glasses that would have turned me to stone had I not flashed her an apologetic grin. "I didn't mean to be disrespectful," I ventured.

"I suppose Woo *is* my daughter, of sorts."

"More like your *familiar*," I said without thinking."

Emily started to laugh at that. "Scottie, you beat all," she said, "but when you're right, you're right."

Woo sidled up to me, angling for a truce, and I began to croon to her: *'love is kinda crazy with a spooky little girl like you'* and she flung her arms about my neck.

"Turncoat," Emily said sharply, but she was smiling. For once all three of us were in harmony. An hour later I couldn't remember why.

I had a vision of greasy, dark water as it lapped the sides of the *Willapa*, its white rails bright against the sunset. A seagull cried the names of the two strangers on deck, chiding Emily and rallying Martyn. The luminous wake of a million phosphorous dolphins sparking fire, followed the wake of the boat and shooting stars fell into the sea, hissing like red-hot horseshoes plunged into icy water.

Fold away all your bright-tinted dresses,
turn the key on your jewels today
and the wealth of your tendril-like tresses
Braid back in a serious way;
no more delicate gloves, no more laces,
no more trifling in boudoir or bower,
but come with your souls in your faces
to meet the stern wants of the hour.

~ from the diary
of an anonymous World War I nurse

Art, Sex,
and Rock & Roll

It was time to grow up, to wear real clothes, to stifle nursery rhymes, and to ride horses bareback like an Amazon warrior. Frilliness couldn't serve art, so Emily roamed the forests and hiked the Indian trails. Her body, her suitors, her rogues, and her sisters – they all crushed in. Doctors called it hysteria, but it was unprocessed love, too passionate to last, too immediate to accept.

I felt Emily's old cold feet failures, and sabotaged any shred of carnal appetite left to me. I had my share of silent romances, like all girls, and felt the sting of waiting in the shadows. Waiting for the proffered hand to offer more than a dance or the eyes sending the suggestion of a tryst. I felt Emily's delicious hint of tingling power. I recognized Martyn's effect on her. I spoke to stop her memories mingling with mine.

"Art is sexual," I said. "Pure biology. Great art is like making love to a canvas."

"And good art? That's a tease," Emily said.

"Nature is sex. Sex is a man and woman's nature," I said. "We exist to procreate. Humans have mating seasons. Women are fertile and ripe and succulent in their turn. Some of us are barren. Spinsters lay fallow. Were you a desert or a forest?" I asked.

Emily was animated. "A woman has to be one or the other, but an artist has to be both. A painting requires a seed. It has to gestate. There are seasons when the ability to make art atrophies. Painting is elemental: fiery passion grounded by the earth.

Cave paintings are the religious fervors of peak moments. The annunciations and crucifixions. Saints in martyrdom. Ceilings and walls of inspiration, temptation, and fear. Only later, did humans create pastoral landscapes to ease the eyes and heart from emotional pain."

"And the ironies of still life," I said. "Flowers and fruit that speak of nothing but decor."

"Not all," Emily offered. "There were themes of 'momento mori' – the paintings of floral arrangements allowed to age and disintegrate. Dead flowers, rotting fruit, and skulls. What was that all about?"

"It was a statement," I said. "I used to think it was the crystallization of grief, but then I studied art history. The sentiment behind them went a lot deeper than that. May it please you to know it stood as a reminder to the living, and especially the famous. *Remember your mortality. Look behind you. Remember that you are but a man. Remember that you'll die.* And here you are, looking ahead, blowing off death. We need a whole new genre of art to express that."

Emily turned and looked out the window. "I liked to sell my paintings from home – straight from the horse's mouth, so to speak," she said.

Emily opened up about being an artist. "I hated writing the artist's statement," she said. "That old chestnut. The synopsis of visual art put into words. Why do galleries make us do that?"

"Galleries are just fancy grocery stores," I said. "Their products are paintings that need labels we call titles. Artist statements are no different from a list of ingredients and calorie content. Art is apples and oranges. The inflated price of a dozen Faberge eggs."

Emily harrumphed, back in the form of her elder self. "I say, if a person can't read a painting, they sure as hell won't understand an artist's statement."

"I experience painting as intimacy," I said. "One has to be tender with a creative idea."

Emily disagreed. "I preferred to be aggressive. Art is a fight to the finish."

"What are you saying? Art has to be a struggle?"

"And you're going to say that concept is another word for conception, and that it's the difference between puppy love and consummated passion?"

"Well, it is," I said. "Some paintings are aborted. One has to paint over a bad relationship of form and color. Canvasses cost too much to throw away."

Emily held her palm out like a stop sign. "Art has to be rejected to make way for new life," she said. "I learned to paint more honestly *and* appreciate love, by making terrible mistakes."

"I guess I still am," I said.

Emily said nothing and shot me a look of concern.

"Well, there are Trudies are everywhere," I said.

"No relationship is smooth sailing," Emily replied, "living alone has its joys, as you well know. You can't beat simple pleasures."

To that, I responded with an upset stomach, ironically known as heartburn.

It was my turn to premise. "You denied that you were juicy in the flesh. What happened to Whitman's influence?"

"I didn't discover Whitman till I was old," Emily said. "He would have shocked me if I had read him earlier."

It was my chance to be as outspoken as Emily. I pretended I was as an uninhibited old woman allowed to blurt anything. "I think you poured yourself on art," I said. "I see you as an elemental painter who stalked art. A huntress who sniffed out the deepest groves where the male trees waited like sturdy sentinels and trapped their masculine appeal. You painted phallic trees: thick robust summer-heavy bad boys, spindly shy-youth saplings, and defiantly-pliable scruffy adolescents.

You stalked the Green Man in all his forms, luring and teasing the gnarled bark-skinned men as well as the smooth supple whippersnappers bending to a girl's wildest dreams on receptive 'salad days'.

I think I know what you were after. Like Merlin's female apprentice, Nimue, you wanted to capture the mystical soul of your master and muse. Your paintings captured the splashes of light that penetrated the forest's secret trysting places and vibrated the chlorophyll into sublime music. You alternated between hunting and haunting with dazzling palettes of compatible color genders."

Emily remained silently contemplating my mood and sentiments, and I continued to hound her about sex and art. If nothing else, I was airing my own opinions while I fished for hers:

"Within your work I sense the organic nature of crevices in the rocks that whisper like painted mouths, expectant as parted lips yearning for the seductive sound of love poetry. Complexions white as thistle silk, and red cherries like warm kisses. V-shaped branches like open legs, sticky with the promise of forbidden love. Smoky moss and clinging fur, pungent with spicy fingers.

The energy of art is the rapid pulse of throb and thumps begging for attention. It seduces. A high of deep connection consummates in a marriage of form and light."

"How do you know what I felt when I painted?" Emily finally interjected, obviously peeved.

"Because your thoughts are inside my head right now. All I can think of is Martyn. All I can see is the word art inside his name. Why is that? What does that mean?"

Emily ignored my question. "It's what one feels born to do," she enthused, "consume the world and reproduce it, fair and free."

"The anthropology of art is iffy. You can play

dead while you're alive or be reborn after you die. When your senses blow wide, it's love. Pure love," I remarked, feeling woozy.

"Scottie, either you're a poet or I am," Emily said, "You know... the seedy sort I once feared."

I had written of the great elusive 'yes' in a work of art. Now it was more. I understood the sheer effort of painting for the multiple hits of creative bliss. I allowed Emily to lecture through me:

> *"One can play with dolls and remain childless. Mummies and daddies, princes and glass slipper games. The universe is a great convulsion that moves planets and shatters stars.*
>
> *Intimacy carries fears. Romance smells good. Vanity, ego, and the blushing need to mate, drives us on. The ranks of chemistry obeys Hydrogen, its own creator. Hydrogen says go forth and combust. Glow, flame, and explode. The same way a forest sparks from lightning, programmed to burn to the ground. Phoenix trees burn from the joy of red to white-hot passion. The final moments of clear-cut death surprise us, and then we are reclaimed in a silent forest of rebirth, reincarnation, and hibernation."*

It was a strange experience being the speaker and the listener at the same time.

Emily was a young woman, with a shocked expression. "Scottie, you wear me out."

I was reeling, but I pressed her. "Birds and bees weren't enough were they?"

Emily was frank. "Birds, dogs and cats, a rat, one elephant, and an enchanted monkey, was almost enough," she answered.

I dreamed of a lush steaming jungle – its tree canopy peppered with leaping, brown monkeys. A 'hundredth monkey' sat apart, eyes closed in meditation, softly chanting woo woo woo as her yellow fur flamed into red through vibrant purple and finally settled on peacock blue. The shriek of the colony behind her fell silent and she opened her eyes. The message in her eyes reached clear across time, *that's my girl*, they said.

Victoria Rules the Waves

f it was good enough for the queen, it was almost an official edict for her subjects in the colonies to immediately follow suit. Victoria's namesake outpost was no exception. Queen V favored authoress Marie Corelli, and women supportively-clad in mourning black obediently succumbed, reading words of love under the covers after dark.

The sovereign Queen declared novels suitable for the frail constitutions of genteel women in need of rigorous cold baths and more robust diets. Women were advised to toughen up after Victoria suffered the loss of her Albert. It seemed only fair.

Corelli stated that love conquered death, and it must have been true, the queen herself read her novels and survived the storms of bereavement to an incredibly old age. Victoria's long reign reeked of death and the black veils of mourning; indeed her majesty had been rather inspired by widowhood.

Royal authority enjoys the powers of city hall many times over. There's no arguing with it, and fighting against it is pointless. Marie wrote of rare love, and so Victoria sanctioned Marie's soapbox, and ironically, Marie's theories of rebirth kept the Queen's hopes of being reunited with her dead husband, alive. Victoria gleaned from Miss Corelli, that Albert's clothes and belongings contained his soul signature and that laying out his shaving things somehow strengthened their waning bond. It could even be argued that Victoria's eccentricities became more predominantly far-fetched as the memory of her husband tried to fade.

When I informed Emily that Mr. Brown, the Queen's subsequent love interest had made her an emotional wreck, Emily said, "We never heard of him."

"I'm no more *amused* than the Queen," Emily sniffed, just to be cantankerous.

"Sure you are," I threw back. "I think that's your defining characteristic. To be amused but to look daggers at the same time."

"I never looked daggers."

"You spoke daggers. You meant daggers. Sometimes the trees you painted looked like daggers," I proclaimed.

Emily's eyes narrowed and she reverted to hairnet Em, and I conceded to her frumpy side.

"The queen reminds me of my mother," Emily said. "Especially those pictures when she wears her tiny diamond crown. Mother would have looked like that, had she lived to old age."

"I always thought Queen Victoria looked like a bloated frog under that thing. Did you know it was purposely designed to accentuate her widow's weeds during her prolonged reign of never-ending bereavement? Suffering seemed to have actually *lengthened* her life."

"She was larger than life," Emily said.

"Your queen screwed-over a generation of cardboard cut-out women," I said. "Victoria, the woman with more power than any man of her time, apparently knew incandescent love, had many healthy babies, and dined on steamy novels three times a day, yet her formal edicts were judgmental suggestions for her people to curtail the indecencies of sexual pleasures and gluttony with modesty. Prude *and* prejudice," I said, and guzzled my bottled water. I lifted it high."Here's to being chased and chaste. In death as in life, till love do us part," I intoned as a tribute. "Maybe it was Victoria and not Marie Antoinette who cried 'let them eat cake' to their citizens," I suggested. "She did invent the Victoria Sponge and could certainly make short work of a dessert trolley."

Like history, victory repeats itself. One has to admire the rigid loyalty of the ghosts of Victorians past for their sheer determination to emotionally survive imperial rules – absolutes which lacked their monarch's 'grace and favor'.

I mused about two contemporary women artists, Emily and a gentle Beatrix Potter, born to the privilege of wealth, so different, yet so alike. Independent, but gentility-crushed, rising over the tyranny of their parent's oppressive values. A couple of nature goddesses: one drawn to the untamed wild of British Columbia, the other to retreat into the pastoral bliss of England's Lake District.

It was landscapes which offered both women sanctuary from bruised hearts. Somehow they survived to inspire the world with genteel and feral visions of nature. Beatrix to comfort childhood; Emily to blaze the trail of primal nature and stir the senses into a sexual fusion. Advocates of an internal feminist movement demonstrated by personal revolutions of eccentric behavior.

Emily and Beatrix Potter – it was amazing that the times produced parallel women artists who grew into strange, lumpy old birds, clutching animals they loved after the disappointments of men and averting motherhood made them desperate. I imagined them sharing tea and animal yarns, churning out eccentricity by the bucketful.

Pleased by their belated successes and perplexed by the sad turns of fate regarding love. Beatrix, lost a love soon after it was found and accepted; Emily, kept a lover interested after firmly rejecting him. Both women found consolation in pet children and by diving into the arts in defiance of the Old Boys who disregarded them so quickly.

It is likely Miss Potter would have found Emily's art disturbing, and Emily openly dismissed the watercolor dreams of traditional painting, as insipid. The pastel Beatrix and the primary colours of Emily would settle on the bonding of animal-to-human as the legacy of their most tender affections.

"Papa said things should be done the Victorian way. The English way, by the Queen's rules."

"Permission to sin, please," I said, tongue-in-cheek.

Emily thought her affection for Martyn had died after fifteen years, but then, out of the blue on a visit to San Francisco, his name was dropped like an unexploded memory into her vulnerable life. Her fears had been too great; the price of marriage had been too high. Her remorse had been palpable. I could feel it as if it were yesterday.

I never saw the boy;
he was there and I knew his name...
... but where he came from
I did not know.

~ Emily Carr ~
The Book of Small

The Garden of Other-Worldly Delights

"Drummie was real," Emily said. "As I once thought, a spirit child. I was four, and Drummie was still in his mother's womb."

I had seen what real time had done to Emily's garden. Her vast symphony of flowering fields were now a chess board of cramped buildings. But she couldn't see it. It kept her mood high to remember her first playground as it had been. As it would always be, to a girl who reigned as its first resident princess and grew to return as its last true queen.

"I want the skinny on Drummie," I announced casually as we pulled away from the gas pump.

Woo checked out the bag of groceries I had bought in the convenient store: candy, bottles of water, two Pink Lady apples, a small bag of Bing cherries and a banana. Woo waved the banana like a sword. "Yes it's for you," I said, and reached to pet her. Hiss she went... chatter, chatter, shriek, *Hands off!*

"Your welcome," I said.

Woo's body language was clear: *Get your own!*

"Why do you think Drummie always averted his face?"

"He didn't. Have you never heard of fairy glamour?"

"I was a kid once, you know. The lore never changes: fairies can erase human memories and appear in disguise. Are you saying your invisible boy was one of them?"

"Don't be ridiculous. He was an unborn child."

"I stand corrected. That's not ridiculous at all."

A banana skin hurled itself at the windshield and left a streak of goo.

I gave Woo a filthy look. "What the hell!"

Her expression came back swiftly: *like I care.*

"Isabella was our proud guardian. She saw everything," Emily recalled dreamily.

"And she was a fairy?"

"She was a grapevine."

"Of course she was."

A hail of cherry pits and stems peppered my hair. "Hey!"

"Woo!" Emily shrieked, for heaven's sake!"

"Isabella was groomed and clipped into perfection," Emily said, "Father named his obsession, Isabella. His free time was happily devoted to Isabella's tresses. Her green locks spilled over our window sills like Rapunzel. She was very cultivated in her green lace frock.

I remember following the sound of Drummie's laughter through the spicy foliage. I heard him call: 'catch me up'.

Time ran like a clear stream, then. We children were the knight and princess of Carr Street. Our kingdom was a garden that stretched from 1875 to a different garden, in 1945, with sombre stone vases and austere columns. I saw it in my dreams all the time and couldn't place it. Do you know where it is? Did I get there?"

Emily's voice changed, the lightness gone.

I changed the subject quickly. "You said you followed him? Drummie?"

"Yes, everywhere. Sometimes we were our normal size, but most of the time we could fit into Dede's old dollhouse, had we been invited."

"I asked Drummie to come inside the kitchen once, and he almost did, but grownup voices startled him and he blew out like a candle. He didn't fade; he was just gone. By the time I was six, he had vanished altogether.

I used to watch him clamber up Isabella's as easily as a ladder until I could only hear his progress as he pushed the glossy leaves aside."

A wet cherrystone hit me in the side of the head. "Thanks Woo."

"Is it okay for her to eat the stems," I asked Emily.

"She eats *beetles*," Emily replied.

"It's fine to indulge in a little childhood fantasy," I said. "Goodness knows it gets kids through visits to the dentist and boring school days, the mumps, and out of a lot of chores. But now? Emily you're..."

"Dead?"

"Does that mean you're no age at all?"

"It means I'm every age I ever was. Things are

coming back to me because I am shifting time. I am not regressing or recreating events. I'm replaying them."

"But dwelling on the poetic realms of an evaporated garden has little to do with a posthumous wedding."

"It has everything to do with Martyn and I," she said. "Memories engage spirit, and there is no greater concentration of spirit than when you're a child. The big world has no claims upon your imagination. As four-year-old Small, I was more *me* than at any other '*size*'."

Emily retrieved the banana peel and teased me. "Shall I give this back to Woo? or are you going to visit Small?"

"Well," she chuckled, "what's it gonna be?"

"Let's have a garden party. Paint me a picture," I said. Make me see it. Make me feel it. I'll follow you."

"You are feeling it, or starting to. Pretty soon you'll be there. You'll be sensible and let go of now."

"Emily, stop scaring me."

"Stop resisting me, then."

Woo grabbed the soggy peel, now turned black, and nibbled on the bitter flesh. It had to taste better than earwigs and cicadas, I thought.

We drove the next few minutes in silence. Both of us needed to isolate our positions.

I knocked on the dashboard three times. A monkey's eyes cast a glance at me: *what?*

"Can Emily come out and play," I asked Woo. She promptly turned her back on me and began to wash her face with the back of her hand.

"That's a yes, then," I said, and turned to Emily. "Take me there."

Emily didn't hesitate, but she grinned a *that's my girl* in my direction. "It's through this foliage curtain. The air is sticky with juice," she began. "Breath it in. The clover. The plums and pears. Can you smell them? Don't answer. Strawberries are almost melting with old age, the topsoil smells of sunshine, mossy perfume lures a few lazy bees. Their wings waft the scent of honey towards us from the golden crystals of pollen and nectar stuck to their legs.

Visualize the colours of Woo: purple lilac, yellow daffodils, orange tiger-lilies, red poppies, bluebells, white Lily of the Valley, and green grass. There are seven. You will see them all."

"I'm with you," I said.

Woo's dress changed to green with red polka dots and Emily pointed to the fabric. "Woo is feeling like a sun-drizzled apple orchard blanketed with windfalls.

The faces you can see in the bark of the cherry tree are watching us. It's all good, they're friendly. Listen and watch. The crackle of burning leaves from the vegetable patch is sending smoke signals. To us, it's a forest fire but we're safe. The winds have picked up its scent of burnt licorice and sent it to Beacon Hill to visit the swans. It makes us hungry for the sweets in my apron pocket."

"Do I have an apron too?"

"Why don't you look"

"I do. It's white. A white cotton pinafore with a ruffle at the bottom."

"Check your pockets," Emily said.

"One super-size gummy bear. It's red."

Emily laughed, "It's you who have shrunken in size. Goody. I have dolly mixtures. Each one is the size of a birthday cake. Lucky for me you love to share. Unicorn tea would be nice. Would you like some?"

"Unicorn tea?"

"It's not hot. It's cold water with milk and sugar," she said.

"But, no tea?"

"Absolutely none."

"But then..." I started to protest.

"Don't think, Scottie. Feel. It's starting to rain, so we take shelter under a terracotta flowerpot. Follow me. Mind your footing through the tendrils and spirals of the fallen leaves. See, the pot has a hole in the bottom and a chipped rim. Be careful, it's sharp. Inside, the lower half is a darker color where the damp has been absorbed. Peep through the hole. Can you see the rain spattering the dappled paving stones thick with moss growing between their toes. The drops jump and leap, turning the red bricks to the colour of burgundy wine."

I glanced over at Emily. In the passenger seat, sat an adorable four-year-old girl wearing a plaid dress. She tossed her ringlets, smiled at me, and said "hello," and I detected the hint of a giggle in her voice.

"Hello," I said back, checking my hands on the steering wheel to make sure they were adult hands and that my feet reached the floor peddles. We were okay. I could drive fine, but, we had been driving so long we might well be anywhere. The car clock said two hours had passed.

"I think I'm done, Small. I just saw a frog wearing a crown."

Woo Woo VERONICA KNOX

"That's Queen Victoria."

"Oh, come on! Give me a break."

"Small laughed, "Scottie, you are so easy to fool."

We stopped for sandwiches and big-girl tea, piping hot with milk and sugar. I closed my eyes for a minute. Woo was toying with the electronic window control. It whined up and down and the sound was a comforting drone. I was on the edge of sleep, when Woo nipped my finger. "Owww! What the hey!" Woo's eyes said: *listen up, pay attention!*

Fog had enveloped the car and Emily was speaking to the white space beyond the windscreen. "I know Drummie was a knight because he rode a white horse, and he faced down dragonflies without a sword. They knelt before him and then took to the air. Once, I was invited to ride. I didn't go. I was getting older and starting to be careful.

It's a good retreat, to shrink in size, as well as from the horrors of growing up and being battered with responsibilities and the realities of life and death. I was made to kiss a dead baby once. Imagine?"

"Ewwww!"

"It was like touching a porcelain doll."

I commented that Victorians were remarkably insensitive for a generation priding themselves on frayed nerves and smelling salts. "Lands of daisy chains and snail coaches are a child's answer to indecent exposure," I said, to the same emptiness of the lost road ahead.

Small was holding Woo's hand as she spoke, "Drummie was Martyn," she said.

As soon as Emily's words were out she grew up twenty years "Now that I am dead, I know who Martyn is. Who *we* were, and why he was so insistent and myself so guarded. I was the leader before he was born and then he ran passed me. We were reading different pages of the same story. He should have waited."

"He did," I said.

I drove another hour to a motel, reflecting on the suspended death sentences of serial rejection. The more miles between Jon and I, Emily became larger than death and I shrivelled into a woman who wanted to retreat into solitude. My phone trilled at 9 p.m. and sent a jolt of nausea through my gut. I answered shaking, but it was a wrong number, so I called Jon instead while Woo stared at me. I misdialled on the first attempt and then got a prompt from a recorded operator: *the number you have dialled is not in service. Please check your directory and try again.*

Emily and Martyn's mind-to-mind combat played itself out to exhaustion on the chessboards of Victoria and Queens Park and San Francisco and soon, San Diego.

The wars of Hampstead Heath and the battleship steamer, *Willapa,* began on the peaceful jousting fields of childhood, where a boy on a white horse won the heart of a fair maiden under fragrant canopies of jasmine and roses, moments before they woke up.

Often at night,
I went to (Woo's) sleeping box
and took one of her soft, warm little fists
cuddled under her chin, in my hand.
She looked at me with sleepy eyes,
yawned, and murmured:
woo, woo.

~ Emily Carr ~

The Monkey's Paw

It's Halloween every day with Woo. This hour, her costume was missing its orange wig, otherwise she looks like Little Orphan Annie on caffeine: a red dress with short sleeves and a white peter pan collar. Her button monkey eyes were all trick and no treat.

Emily had my complete undivided attention. She could spin a yarn like a sailor tying knots, but I was anticipating her words.

"Some days there were too many Williams," Emily said. "The day I met Agnes Jacobs she looked like a painting, I saw her face framed in sunshine. Fresh motherhood suited her. She was the classic English rose, brimming with life, and I was enchanted to have a new friend. Unusual for me. The King's Place Road in London's east end became a delightful and regular destination.

It was 1901, and Agnes was searching for an art student. I had been recommended. Her author

-husband, William, needed an illustrator. Would I consider showing him some samples of my work? His regular partner (another William) was overrun by commercial deadlines? Agnes tiptoed around and over her mission for her husband's new book. I could see it peeping out from her infant's pram. All I could think of, was that a baby carriage was a practical device – a woman's wheel barrow for carrying art supplies and shopping, if one hadn't a baby to push. From that moment, I coveted one of my own.

Agnes had brought me a slim volume of short stories, and I thanked her prettily and remarked how beautiful her rather plain baby girl was.

Her husband's next book was in the galley stage and required half a dozen drawings. Pen and ink, no color. The plates were too expensive.

I meant to keep in touch, but Agnes was overwhelmed by wifely duties as much as I was art's willing slave. Our taskmasters separated us quickly.

William Wymark Jacobs had a macabre streak. I managed to read one story which captivated and repulsed me. It put me off monkeys all together, and I had a great affinity for them, which you and I can discuss later. *The Monkey's Paw* left an indelible streak of blood in my mind, but it got me back to the London Zoo, where I sketched the gibbons for hours. I was enchanted by their button eyes asking so many questions. Martyn and I had been there on one of his asking days.

Martyn had asked me to marry him, for the hundredth time, with the monkeys whooping in the background. I knew what he was about; I received his proposals several times a week. I watched the monkeys over his shoulder when he hugged me, and one of them flew into paroxysms of joy. I closed my eyes, blocking its happiness. I felt only sadness. I couldn't say yes, and by saying no, Martyn would disappear out of my world. Either answer spelled loss. I felt I couldn't bear such pain. But that was the very spot where I had bottled up all my feelings and said goodbye to Martyn on his last day in London. Everything changed in front of that cage and those carefree creatures. Martyn sailed for Canada and I blindly threw myself into a nervous breakdown.

I stayed to watch the chimps tea party, which made me thirsty and hungry for cake and bought a small tin monkey that hopped when wound up to remind me of that little dance of merriment. I had envied the creature's ability to experience happiness even in captivity. She was wearing a dress. Her cage seemed protective rather than a restriction. Playing monkey games was all she had to do, marriage was out of the question. I told her she was a lucky girl."

"An amazing premonition," I said.

"Pardon?"

"Your link with the monkeys. It was very woo-woo," I said."

"How?"

"Spooky, clairvoyant, soul recognition. Woo is clearly your familiar, your creature."

Emily sighed. "I mustn't discuss that right now."

"Later then, if it's so taboo. Timing is everything."

The notion pleased her. "Yes, after the whole thing's over." Emily steered us into a related topic.

Woo kept bringing me that ivory elephant whenever I got cabin fever. She placed it where I couldn't miss it. I think she meant it was time for us to go camping."

"You already told me she did that," I reminded her.

"You must have heard that from somebody else," she said.

Maybe I had. I was confused. Had Emily told me or had I simply remembered her own thoughts?

I wanted every moment of Paris for art.
I wanted, now, to find out what this
'New Art' was all about.

~ Emily Carr ~

First Impressions;
Lasting Influence

mily had been desperate to find the 'New Art' she'd heard about.

"I tried to explain the art of the Impressionists to my sisters," Emily said. "They had brittle minds. I planted seeds of art for them but they were barren soil."

"Art is in the seeing," I said.

"Well, I *told* it!"

"There's no need to snap at me. Tell me the way you told them," I suggested. "I'll pretend I know nothing."

Emily looked up and around for a place to begin. "If you drop a cake iced with flowers and words, and it falls face-down on the floor, and you push it hard into the linoleum, and turn it 45 degrees to blur the pink roses into the green happy birthday..." Emily paused to see if I was following, I nodded for her to continue.

Emily mimed scooping up the cake, depositing it on a platter. She swept her hands over it, smooshing it together. "And if you mashed it flat, knifing the icing from chaos to order, and smoothed over the fault lines, it would be an impressionist painting of an English garden."

"Now, why can't all art lessons be that simple?" I asked. "I can't believe your sisters weren't enlightened. That was a brilliant lecture. Thank you."

"Our garden looked like that," she said. "Father planted chaos on purpose. It was the English way."

The Latin quarter of Paris soon offered Emily riots of unorthodox colour, country light, and quaint forms. Clear hot reds brushed against sunshine yellows and bright blues challenged pure orange in a battle for supremacy. The arguments flourished on the canvas into an agreement of brilliant landscapes. Emily played like a child with finger-paints, forgetting to be tidy, jumping over the rules of watercolor and insipid charcoal and Chinese Red conté crayon.

The colours of France travelled back with Emily, over the Atlantic Ocean and across Canada to the Pacific coast. Unbeknownst to Emily, she had passed through the art belt of Ontario without an inkling of her future.

"How ya gonna keep em down on the farm after they've seen Pareeeee?" I said.

Emily wheezed a heavy laugh. "Beats me."

"Paris can be spelled with five e's," I said.

I am convinced
that especially in strange environments,
monkeys select a background
as near to their own colour as possible.

~ Emily Carr ~

Mrs. Noah

"Only two?" Emily questioned. Noah couldn't have heard God right. He must have needed a hearing aid."

"I daresay, your God knew a thing or three about proliferation of the species," I said.

An indignant Emily faced me. "He isn't mine, and there's no need to rub it in Scottie."

"Well, in relation to my personal acquaintance with *Him*, he *is* yours."

"Relationships with the Almighty are awkward. Come to think of it, so are the one's with the sons of Adam."

"I have to say I'm grateful to have only *one* monkey in my car. A pair would be disgusting."

"Nothing personal, Woo," Emily said.

"Speak for yourself," I said, and addressed Woo in my rear-view mirror. "You are *one* royal pain in the arse." I made a display of emphasizing the word, *one*. I think she said *bite me* in monk-speak. So much for speak-no-evil.

Woo tried her best to stick out her tongue, but her simian bone structure lacked the necessary facial muscles for copying the motion I had sent her.

I gave her an example of a Bronx cheer. I was tired of being pushed around by a Javanese pipsqueak.

It was going on for the October-dark of 6 pm when I pulled over. Navigation required a whole other talent when driving through a city. I pored over the map with a cobalt-blue flashlight the size of a large fountain pen.

Woo wanted it. She started her *give me* dance, so I turned the light directly on her dress to amuse her, and was startled to see the spot where the light touched her was a kaleidoscope of pulsating colours. Very like an artist's messy palette, but also, terrifyingly like the entrance to an hypnotic tunnel. I fancied it would lure me in and I looked away.

A delicate monkey finger reached under my arm and delicately touched the plastic surface of the map. It pointed to where we were, then it traced a route to where we wanted to be. *Woo woo woo* chirped the adorable version of Woo's voice. She looked deceivingly innocent, her expression vacant as an atheist's prayer.

Woo's reward was my red backup penlight with the batteries removed, but she grew tired of switching it on with no beam and opened the end to see if the light was inside. She gave me a filthy look after she tipped it upside-down and nothing appeared.

I shrugged a 'sorry, that's tough'. Emily cackled, she was old again.

"You should stay the bride to be," I suggested.

"I thought I was," she said.

We were lost, so I suggested we send out our resident compass to assess the lay of the land, disguised as an olive-branch. While Woo leapt at the chance, we discussed her.

"I was going to name Woo, Jemima," Emily said, "but she named herself. The first sound I heard her utter when I got her home was, 'woo woo woo'. It stuck."

"Did you name your dog Billy for William?"

"I did. How clever of you to guess."

"I'm a research detective. Have we met?"

"Still, you ask the obscure questions. That's a talent."

"Well, thank you, but I just ask every question that pops into my head. Gathering useless trivia often leads to buried treasure."

"There's no end to words that hint of death, is there?"

"Right now we're programmed to hear them, that's all."

"Who is Jenner named after?"

"A Scottish department store."

"All right, don't tell me. I was making conversation."

"It's a store in Edinburgh, where my grandmother used to work when she was the age I am now. When I first saw Jenner in the animal shelter, he was chewing a Black Watch tartan blanket, like the one I bought as a souvenir of Scotland. The name Jenner appeared on my tongue, so I used it."

I wrote in my journal:

> *'Emily isn't hard to analyse, but*
> *she knows this, and since she can*
> *read my mind, I am writing this on*

purpose. *I want her to know what I have come to believe. I think that work became her substitute beloved, and because repressing her sexual nature pushed her landscapes into a subliminal masculine perspective, the act of painting frustrated as often as it satisfied. Passion for a male companion remained no matter how busy she made herself. She threw herself into projects that devoured her time. Guilt was disguised as hysteria. Her collective patterns of pride, shame, defiance, and longing, made her ill.*

Toughness was a Canadian trait she celebrated to her physical detriment. She was strong, yes, but not the indestructible persona she liked to promote in public. She witnessed the hardships of her native acquaintances and measured her life experiences against their spirit. It annoyed her that she couldn't be that kind of resilient. She set herself hardships that were adventurous and her penchant for eccentricity sparked a reputation she could live with in her memoirs.

For certain it was her memoirs that were burned so ferociously when times were bad. And there were many of those. The companionship of her sisters was a blessing

WooWoo VERONICA KNOX

and a curse. She had no creative
support, but what the threesome
lacked in compassion they gained
in solidarity. Old biddies, sharing chores in defiance of popular
opinion. Lizzie hear-no-evil, Alice
speak-no-evil, and Emily see-no-
evil. Cantankerous was Emily's island of refuge. A few were allowed
to visit. Woo, the fourth monkey of
spare-no-evil, matched the criteri-
on perfectly.

Emily was a formidable work-
aholic for a reason. She blamed it
on 'needs must' but nothing that
intense is a fluke, and nothing
could disguise her physical needs
calling behind the phallic trees
she painted. In fact, they probably reminded her of what she was
missing. Emily turned her back
on love and painting for years at
a time. She was overwhelmed by
long periods of financial hardship.
There were moments of creative
joy, but nothing to sustain her for
long. She was a searcher. Beyond
was the place she wanted. How
she yearned to reach it. For a long
time she was at sixes and sevens
making ends meet in an atmosphere of depression and war.

Art did energize Emily and in
her last years she gained confidence

and confidants, but birds and dogs kept most of her loneliness in check. Then, Woo arrived and let in a blast of winter power. Emily felt revived from the shock. It was time to face the promises she had made, but too late for romance. Her last relationships were sounding boards of tender friendships, but even then, when she was alone, her world closed about her whispering of failure. She haunted herself. She wrote to feel what she had lost – to feel she wasn't a 'done'.

How do I know any of this? I am more Emily than Scottie, now. I'm in danger of disappearing so far into another's psyche, I may never get home. If home is where the heart is, maybe it's me who is a 'done'.

In her own words, Emily divulged some secrets, but she didn't have to; I could feel them under my skin. I could see the figure of Drummie his little face eclipsed by a shaft of light. Sunbeams were his allies, but it was Emily's consciousness that conjured them in order to protect herself from seeing too clearly. So many excuses. Are my words also hers?

"Beyond the old garden fence, I sensed a 'him' when I was a child. My invisible boy, Drummie, always waiting, always loyal and

Woo Woo VERONICA KNOX

kind. Our companionship made a mockery of the relationship prisons of our elders, but we would marry, he said. He even knew where.

Drummie showed me the corner of the garden where it would be, and described the mauve gown I would wear. It was the innocent play-house-marriage of children, but with knowledge of more. I trusted him completely. I loved him completely.

He never grew old as I did. My Peter Pan visited me for a few months. We went riding on white horses and made daisy chains. We picnicked on lemon barley-water and arrowroot biscuits, and fruit from our orchard. We gathered lilacs and posies of pretty weeds, and once, Drummie made me a bouquet of bare branches that Lizzie threw out, while I slept.

Then Drummie said he had to go away for a while and that he would be back. I waited and waited. I was still waiting when I had a dream of him in 1933. I was sixty-two by then. That was the last time I saw him, well, I never truly ever saw his face, but it didn't matter. Drummie was Drummie, and we loved without question, the untainted love of innocence."

Emily (and I ?) had waited for a love that could measure up to Drummie, and in the meantime, the Carr's garden provided a veritable farm for 'Small'. First the family cow and carriage horses, and then the English jungle creatures: chickens, ducks, guinea fowl, and songbirds. 'Youth' collected Parakeets, budgies, wild songbirds, a peacock, and a crow. 'Middle-age' filled kennels with Old English Sheepdogs and Griffons and an Irish Wolfhound named Jenner, (or was that me?) There were more competitive birds: Sally, a white cockatoo, and a bright parrot named Jane. A veritable gaggle of life-forms kept her (me) busy. An arc of litters, colonies, singular orphans and other fauna paraded in and out of Emily's revolving circus. I heard the names Dolly and Luke fretting somewhere in my past, (I couldn't remember where). There were ever-present cats, one rat, and finally, 'Old-Age' found a Java monkey. One wonders, could unicorns have been far behind? Is my future too far ahead to understand?

Emily denied my suggestion: "Married to my work? Hogwash!" she said.

"You were a farmer," I added. I can see you. Raking, planting, weeding, feeding animals and birds in all kinds of weather. Muddy work boots. Gloves with no fingers. Shovelling coal, hauling wood, turning compost piles, digging for clay. I see you burning leaves and firing up a backyard kiln to bake pots. I can feel the roughness of your work hands. Shaping, scrubbing, building. You were no stranger to hard labour."

"I was just strange. Leave it at that," Emily said.

"Yesterday is ceasing to exist," I said. "I'm afraid of forgetting my life choked by a hundred years of your roots."

WooWoo   VERONICA KNOX

"I send you my very dear love."
(Martyn remembering the girl in her twenties
who is now in her sixties)

~ Emily Carr ~
Hundreds and Thousands
1936

Bonfire of the Flatteries

here comes a time in everyone's life for a good burning. Burning desires, burning ideas, silent passions, hot diaries and old flames. The lot must go. Psychic arson demands it. It's the great cleansing before the ultimate end of sentient mistakes.

Mis-tales, misdeeds, and misadventures as well as missed dreams.

Emily said that the aftermath of life required pruning, as though it mattered to an omniscient almighty. Whatever one's deeds, the tree of life must become a bonsai of perfection, edited enough to squeeze under the locked pearly gates. Blemishes were snipped into a topiary life of exemplary behaviour, according to the day.

"Why did you destroy your letters and diaries?" I blurted. "What was the point of keeping memories for fifty years and then turning them to ash? Obviously they mattered. What was there to be ashamed of? You weren't going to be around to be lynched in the press."

"I was just wallowing in my biog, and even letters can die of old age. I coffined some. One cremates and buries the dead; I did both," Emily explained.

"You're forgetting the shoebox. You didn't burn that, and you're not letting Martyn rest in peace, now."

"He's *not* at peace. That's why I called you."

"Well, he's not going anywhere, but we, the public, the friends you never met, we are mystified. We care. We're a little miffed at the evasion."

"One does what one does and that's that. No-one has a right to tell me I was wrong."

"Emily, you were wrong."

"I don't recall giving that nun my treasure box. What was her name? Perhaps it was done under Woo's influence. The kind of love I'm talking about can't die, but I have to make amends. It was my turn to love and I turned-tail on it."

I was sure of one thing: the statute of limitations was eternal. Men and women separated from love by determination or fate in the days when showing an ankle was tantamount to indecent exposure meant unrequited love could last a lifetime.

My house was known
as the monkey-house.

~ Emily Carr ~

You, Monkey... M.E. Mule

"Everlasting damn and bother!" Emily cursed. "Something still feels wrong. But that's my life. Love is more than half pain. What's done is done."

"What brought that on? You sound like Eeyore," I said, "his depression was sweetly-morbid too."

"It's just the way I am. It's me. - M. E. Millie-Emily Carr. Me. Mule-headed old me. Stubborn as a donkey. Always was. Still am."

"Miss Woo is a tad stubborn as well."

"She gets it from me."

"So you two *are* related, then."

"In a manner of speaking. I'm Woo's mail order human. I called her to me just before the Indians named me Klee Wyck. The First Nations people taught me all about animal totems and their power. Meeting my animal guide was the first step."

"And you called Woo?"

"Not right away. An elder charged me to tie a cloth banner in an ancient pine to honour the spirits of the trees and thank the ancestors in advance for my name. I had a lovely red silk scarf with me and I used that. Then the shaman bid me make a medicine bundle of things which spoke to me of power. One thing each, of the air and fire and earth and water. I chose a gull's feather, the core of a battered seashell, and a claw-shaped root of a pine tree that seemed oddly familiar.

I made a hollow fire-pit no bigger than a dinner plate, encircled it with large flat stones, and laid a tiny fire that doubled as a medicine wheel. I placed my sacred objects on the north south and east positions and sprinkled them with pipe tobacco, but I was stubborn, and romantically left the direction west empty to represent how I felt after leaving Martyn. I performed a smudge ceremony and closed my eyes, sitting cross-legged by the shore until a profound stillness entered me, absolutely. I let go all resistance and embraced the sound of the tide as it washed towards me over the pebbles, and followed it back out to sea.

"Wait. Feather - air, seashell - water, and root - earth. That's only three. What about fire?"

"I had a page to burn that I'd written in my journal. It was a fiery declaration of my love for Martyn. By the way, the root resembled a monkey's paw, but that escaped my notice at the time.

"Emily, you burned Martyn's name," I accused. "Didn't you realize what you were doing?"

"It was *good* fire," she said. "Symbolic of the wilderness. I claimed a clean start. The way a forest fire clears the path for new growth. My name Klee Wyck came through a ritual fire."

"Everyone comes from a tribe," I said. "The First Nations may be a tad closer to nature. Well, they were in *your* day, but our European names hold power too."

"The cry of a lone seagull led me into my quest."

I blanched when Emily said Seagull. Then I

shrugged it off; gulls were a common sight and sound on the island.

Emily saw my reaction and continued dreamily. "My soul filled up with the pungent scent of pine resin and wood smoke, and I thought of Drummie, because the Indians were beating a rhythm in the settlement behind me.

"Don't you see?" I ranted. "You sacrificed Martyn! You sacrificed love.

Symbols have power, and you were dabbling in the supernatural, wide open to forces you knew nothing about, other than it felt *romantic*."

"My shaman had directed me to open my eyes when ready and observe my surroundings patiently, and the first animal I saw would be for me. I heard the clicking of a squirrel scolding, but it sounded like laughter, and I felt sure that was my animal. When I opened my eyes the forest had disappeared. I sat in a barren landscape of bizarre colours. Nothing broke the distant horizon but the silhouette of a single baobab tree, and the sky was dancing. I could see a thin ribbon of red trailing from a low branch.

I stood and surveyed a beach of bright blue sand. Northern lights flashed in an aura about the crown of the tree like a fire opal. As I got closer to the tree, a solar wind started to buzz softly with static electricity and my skin tingled with ozone.

The trunk of the tree was deep Egyptian purple and got lighter until the uppermost branches were magenta and the leaves were a pale mauve crown. Suddenly the ground changed it's season to sky-blue snow and the branches were bare, shimmering with beads of ice like pearls. A balmy winter Chinook blew me closer to the tree until I could touch the bark. I greeted it and lay down under it to sleep, and then the scene went white as a blank canvas and I met an albino she-monkey, the colour of ivory.

"It wasn't Woo?"

"No. It was Woo's group soul - a spirit creature that whooped with laughter.

"Maybe *she* was the 'laughing one'," I suggested.

"She dropped without making a sound from the center where the leaves had been and landed in front of me. I met her eyes. They were like wise little stars. All my cares left me and I felt I was home. Protected. But then my emotions became as erratic as the aurora borealis. They passed through me one-by-one, and as they did, the monkey's fur changed colour. I think the incident with Martyn beside the monkey house in London Zoo was the first sending from my guide, but I was feeling sorry for myself and ignored it. I experienced a breakdown of communication within myself that night. My nervous system was on fire. I discovered later, that dismissing one's guide is disrespectful enough to cause a physiological great rift for both parties."

"Maybe even a psychological quake."

"It was the last time Martyn ever asked me to marry him."

"It's hardly coincidental that Woo's name means to court romantically," I said. "Don't you think?"

"*That* Missy, is the crux of our relationship. Woo is the quintessential matchmaker. Of course, I didn't know that's what I wanted at the time. Wishers never know the details do they? Woo takes her calling seriously. I'm still under some sort of influence to her."

Woo Woo   VERONICA KNOX

"I believe in layman's terms it's called a spell."

"Woo is a child."

"A poltergeist then. Jon told me about them. They're pesky little tricksters."

"She's playful. God made monkeys that way."

"Woo woo, also means supernatural," I said. "Perhaps you sold your soul to her."

"I think Woo may even have been on crows' nest duty the night I met Martyn."

"Oh, I think you can count on that," I said. "I wonder why didn't she announce *iceberg ahead* in her inimitable 'Cassandra' screech?"

"She had her reasons. Maybe she didn't want to scare me. Shamans and totems work in mysterious ways. Woo doesn't traffic in doom."

"You could have fooled me!"

"I have, several times."

"So, Woo is more than just a native animal guide and now I understand what you meant by calling her a compass? She may even be *your* conscience. She's a regular little Jiminy cricket, hopping all over the place." Which explains why you're so jumpy when Woo's playing matriarch.

"Scottie sometimes you're impossible to follow."

"Surely you remember JC's advice: *Always let your conscience be your guide,* or in our case, navigator. It's rather poetic when you think about it."

"Woo loves poetry," Emily volunteered suddenly.

"Keats or Browning?" I asked, hoping to catch Emily out.

"Lewis Carroll," Emily replied without missing a beat.

"That makes sense. Lewis Carroll wrote: *sometimes I believe in as many as six impossible things before breakfast.* I think he might have been onto something there."

Woo turned lime green which softened to emerald. She flickered like a June-bug.

"Okay then, what's with the monkey chameleon-thing?"

"Woo can't help changing colour. Spirit forms are sensitive to the emotions surrounding them. You know about colour theory. Humans respond to color. Monkeys respond to us. You and I are in a state of flux, so Woo is too."

"Does green mean one of us is jealous?"

Emily's smile was disturbing. She reached over, brazenly took my pen and journal, scribbled a note, and handed it to me with raised eyebrows. She had written: "W.E. are."

"What jealous or in a state of flux?" I asked. "Wait. No need to answer that."

A celebratory, simian Woo-hoo! rang in the woods, and Woo returned triumphant with a handful of beetles. As she cracked each one like a nut, I started to think a terrible thought. That Emily was trying to get out of a contract with Woo and leave me in her place. It was an irrational explanation, but at least I was lucid enough to know it was irrational.

Nothing so delighted (Woo)
as for me to play 'this little piggy went to market'
with her fingers and toes.

~ Emily Carr ~

Monkeys are a Girl's Best Friend

The Motel Six in Seaside, Oregon, was cozy enough, but I was too tired to sleep and as had become our custom, my conversations with Emily served to pass the time. Tonight I drew inspiration from a book about antique toys I'd brought along for just such a moment. There was more to learn about the definitive upper class Victorian childhood.

"I hate these miniature grotesques," I said, showing Emily an illustration from the book. Earlier, in the car we had discussed the Victorian society's morbid obsession with taxidermy. Woo had been throwing croutons at me and I had threatened to turn her into a lamp.

The art of displaying small stuffed creatures wearing clothes seemed to be contagious. It had been all the rage. Dead birds under bell-jars as ornaments, and dioramas of frogs and field mice costumed and posed into eternal servitude, sealed in their own greenhouses. They represented the macabre side of natural history, as if Beatrix Potter had banished her animal characters to miniature chambers of horror in a waxwork museum.

Years ago as an art student, I had seen shelves of the wretched terrariums in the Victoria & Albert Museum. Schoolmarm frogs beating mouse pupils with hawthorn twitches, stern father frogs doling out punishments, boy mice sitting in corners wearing dunce caps, baby mice pushed by froggy nannies – all nightmare material. But then, Victorian dolls were frightening enough - porcelain faces of staring monsters usually with one of the moveable eyelids jammed shut for effect. Golliwogs were especially alarming.

"They were neither cuddly nor educational," I said, "unless one views corporeal punishment as lessons in virtuous behavior. What were they thinking? That it would inspire children?" I asked."

"Hardly that. It was a strange, sad combination of fear and amusement," Emily said. "Spare the rod and all that. Children and mothers had no power. Once, when I had a fearful toothache, the dentist told father I required a couple of fillings. My father said 'nonsense, pull them all out' and so I had several extractions over the dentist's and my mother's protestations. Father's word was law."

"Discipline was a big deal, and impressively ineffective, considering its frequency," I commented.

"Spoiling a child was a considered an offense against religion and commonsense."

"Surely toddlers were spared," I said, hopefully.

"Define toddler," she said.

"Homo Sapien children in the first stages of upright mobility."

"Father rapped our toddler knuckles with a spoon when we fidgeted during bible readings. He had a special wooden ruler for worse offenses. Then

WooWoo VERONICA KNOX

a strap when we were older. Punishments were progressively tougher."

"I rest my case. No wonder children grew up resenting confinement. It's unclear to me, why there wasn't a rush of wild behavior after turning twenty-one."

"Sometimes there was. There were subtle ways to take one's revenge. Mostly, by then, we were browbeaten to obey under the rules of our dear Queen, the namesake of our city – mother of decency, modesty, and restraint."

"Restraint! The woman had *nine* children," I gasped.

"So did my mother."

"Define restraint," I said.

"Holding back one's truth for social points."

"When it comes to poetry and matchmaking, monkeys are smarter than frogs," I said, and quoted *The frog he would a-wooing go* from the book. "Quite nasty really."

"Silly amphibian was gobbled by a goose," Emily interjected. "Serves him right, courting a different species. I was made to recite that one with gestures."

"What alarming offspring a father frog and mother mouse would have created," I said. "Although it would explain a lot about the kids in my kindergarten class who ate glue sticks and sniffed magic markers. I am going to have nightmares."

I realized the ridiculous statement I had uttered, sitting in a bleak motel room with a deceased woman and a monkey who sometimes seemed like an imp from hell.

"I didn't like girly dolls," Emily confessed. "I had a collection of stuffed animals. I had a bruin on wheels, big as a dog. And a leather rocking horse - a dappled grey beauty named Dobbs, with a red harness and a real horsehair mane. I kept him well-groomed."

"I love those Victorian four-legged bears," I said. "Much cooler than rocking horses. They made bears that rocked as well didn't they?"

"Mostly, my toys were live animals, and of course, I had Drummie. After he left I still had him locked away in my imagination. I never felt alone until I was six."

Woo eyed my book. I gestured for her to approach and showed her the picture of a wind-up tin monkey with cymbals, wearing a red fez. She chattered back a reasonable imitation of its grimace before tearing out the page and throwing it in my face. Woo's expression was unbridled contempt.

"I think she just told you to *get stuffed,*" Emily laughed.

Marmie was back in Woo's clutches and I complained to Emily. "If Woo doesn't stop nattering to Marmie, I'm going to go mad!"

"You must *restrain* yourself," Emily said, slyly. "We have a long drive tomorrow."

Woo's investigations were never superficial.
Every object must be felt, smelt, tasted,
pulled to pieces before her curiosity was satisfied.
Only when she had completely wrecked a thing
did she toss it away as having no more interest.

~ Emily Carr ~

My Little Eye

E mily started the game before breakfast. "Something beginning with T," she suggested.

"Trouble?"

"Trouble, my eye!" Emily complained. "Can't we begin the day with something positive?"

"I can do neutral," I said. "I had a bad night. Jon didn't call. I'm too upset to be positive. I really don't want to play word games. I have a headache."

My present situation was disturbing, but I wasn't scared. I felt more displaced than I let on. I observed, even know-it-all ghosts tell lies when they want something. Saying 'boo' a few times just doesn't have the same impact after one is weaned on special-effects and surround sound. A love interest who has suddenly gone silent was scarier.

"Call him," Emily suggested.

"I was stupid to think Jon and I were equal or compatible. He's out of my league."

"Nonsense, that's what I used to say as an excuse when I felt inadequate."

"You mean jealous?"

"I *mean* insignificant."

"Ever since you started to tell me about your past I've been feeling that way. It's called transference. I don't know where my emotions end and yours begin."

"That's an unavoidable side-effect I'm afraid," Emily confessed. "I've had to draw strength from you. I couldn't face this journey without your confidence."

I was horrified. "You're talking about possession."

"That's such an ugly word."

I was outraged. "It's an ugly deed, Millie."

"It's part of our deal."

"No, no, no. It most certainly was not!"

"I told you this would happen."

"Nothing was mentioned about vision sharing or draining my energy or implanting your thoughts."

"Woo mentioned it could happen."

"She can't talk to me Emily. Only you can. Now my self esteem has vanished and all I want to do is hide. I want to be alone. Sometimes, I don't even care if I ever see Jon again."

"I remember that feeling," Emily said.

I pulled into a drive-through and ordered a Mexican salad with chilli on the side. Woo chirruped in Emily's ear.

"Woo wants to know what she's getting?" Emily said.

"There will, on no account, be monkey fingers in my lettuce," I said. "And no way is she getting any chilli."

Emily held Woo's paw up for inspection. "Woo's hands are always clean."

"Make that a cherry and earwig platter," I yelled into the speaker to distract Emily.

The garbled voice seemed perplexed: "Excuse me? Can you repeat that?"

"Sorry, I meant a small side-salad with cherry tomatoes, hold the onions, and an extra packet of croutons. Do you have any kiddie promotions today?"

"We've got some plastic puzzles. I think there's four kinds. There's a kind of Rubik's cube thing," she said.

"Throw in a long-stemmed red rose and a couple of those Rubik's, thanks."

Emily wanted hot milk with honey, so I ordered her hot chocolate, the nearest thing. Woo had the puzzles in pieces before I finished my salad, but it kept her from stealing my lettuce. Why I gave her more croutons is a mystery.

I let Emily prattle. She was nervous, seemingly picking up random memories and excuses, sometimes falling into silence, and other times blurting out her latest thought.

I half-listened to her latest spiel. I was searching for a turn off, reading the coordinates of a map in my head. Some navigator Woo turned out to be.

I think Emily spoke directly to Woo so I would overhear: "We were juicy misinformed young things, waiting to be picked like peaches on the happy-ever-after vine. All around me lay the abandoned shells and dry cores of once-ripe women. Ravished. Deflowered."

Emily was in a trancelike state. She continued: "The markets of procreation were rife with the buying and selling of virginity and genetics and pedigree."

"Why are you telling Woo this?" I asked her.

"I wasn't. She was telling me. I was merely relaying her message to you."

"Woo is clairvoyant?"

"Woo is my third eye. A natural seer."

"Well, that explains a lot," I said. She's certainly a lousy compass. So much for her centering ritual."

"Sarcasm, missy, is the lowest form of ..."

"What? Navigation? Sarcasm, Millie, is the only way I can process statements like the one you just made. I am *not* laughing. Nothing is remotely funny. I can actually feel myself unravelling. I can't keep my food down. I can't sleep."

"Woo knows things."

"Except where we are. So much for ESP. Woo is supposed to be a GPS!"

"Sarcasm is so unattractive," Emily said.

My answer was a fastball, "so are hairnets."

Woo screeched and let a cherry tomato fly that bounced off my forehead, where my headband would have been, had I worn one.

"Cute," I said. Very cute."

"She's actually on your side," Emily said.

Emily freaked me out when she began to narrate her thoughts like she was recording a speech into a tape recorder. She stared into the road ahead and spoke clearly without emotion: "In 1889, the air was choked with love; the ground was littered with trampled hearts and expectations, from being ignored to drowned in courtship. It was overwhelming. My ideal was a perfect man composed of the best attributes of each suitor I met. I had all the time in the world and a narrow window in which to wave them goodbye or invite them to stay. It was all or nothing. No long engagements, just mellow friendships, but I was expected to respond as a woman of the world, ready to make a choice and too many choices hurt my head."

It was becoming clear that Emily's men became a 'blursion' (her term for blurred vision) of demanding voices and arms and kisses. Martyn had been lost in the crowd.

She confessed to me in a candid moment; "I was not courted but hunted, and I felt I had to throw them all over or be eaten alive."

The markets of procreation: the brash buying and selling of sweet young things, must have pitted hard against fate and the soft-flesh of girlhood. Emily's conscience had split down the middle in order to cope. She had made herself ill.

I knew Emily's tortured conscience was a genie in a bottle waiting to explode, because that's how I was beginning to feel. Her recurring affliction diagnosed as 'female hysteria', stopped stalking me and entered my psyche, all nerves firing. The volcano of the magic lamp manifested as an emotional breakdown, and left me in a state of nervous collapse in control of a speeding car.

Our 'Carr-ride to heaven' detoured through hell at each state line, with my nerves popping in erratic bursts of tension and excitement. I tried to focus on the bumper sticker messages of my mother's New-Age books, which implied fear and excitement were the same thing and that one should interchange them on demand when faced with a crisis and sail on through to Neverland. I was on a deserted road with a surreal task – about to chaperone a post-humous reunion, perhaps with a reluctant unco-operative, ex-beau.

I heard the tension in Jon's recorded voice. I called him a half a dozen times in a row leaving a progres-sively more frantic message each time. I heard my voice begging like a desperate stranger. I couldn't stop being needy. Then it got worse. Palpitations in-formed me I was having a panic attack. I liked myself better when I was just angry.

"This is your hysteria isn't it?" I shouted to Emi-ly's profile.

"I was like that for years," she answered, looking straight ahead.

"You have to stop releasing it. I'm experiencing terribly self-destructive thoughts. That's you too isn't it? If I died would it be easier for you?"

"Now you're paranoid," Emily said.

"But you *are* feeling better aren't you?"

"Scottie," Emily said, meekly, "I didn't know it would be this bad."

"No," I said, "but I bet Woo did."

Suddenly, I wanted her —
I wanted her tremendously.
Of course I wasn't going to buy a monkey,
but I asked, what is her price?
My voice went squeaky with wanting.

~ Emily Carr ~

The Nearness of Woo

"Woo seems to have an overabundance of chi," I said, trying to be diplomatic. Woo was getting wilder. She removed a disc of meditation music from my DVD player and flipped it out the window. She wanted jazz and messed with the radio dials until I wanted to throttle her.

Emily had misheard me, "Woo loves cheese," she said.

While Woo played inside Emily's daydreams, jungle rhythms beat an SOS in my brain. The *well, you finally heard me* message.

"No more dresses for Woo," I said to Emily. "You need to make her a straightjacket."

The voice of Woo flowed through the car as an hysterical mantra: "*woo is me, woe woe, woo woo, whoopty doo* and looped to a circle of *woo is me*, again. Sometimes Woo was an interfering busybody – the village matchmaker with a grumpy headache.

"She's reliving my breakdowns," Emily said.
"Why?"

"So I don't have to."

"What about me? You said Woo was on my side."

"You aren't the one putting their afterlife on the line," Emily said.

I surmised it was Woo's job to create chaos. The sort of chaos necessary to push humans into the red zone, where they would be senseless enough to turn off their inhibitions. At least that was my educated guess. Woo was a spectacle of fluctuating rainbow colors, flashing like a traffic light – a monkey slot machine after a jackpot. She settled on fire engine red.

Woo was wearing me out. I put on my sunglasses and she tried to rip them off. I brushed her away on her next attempt and she went dervish crazy.

"Emily keep her away from me," I shouted. "It's not safe to drive."

Emily shrieked, "CUT IT OUT RIGHT NOW!" And Woo responded by flopping into a small heap of nattering agitation. At least she was out of my hair.

Madame Woo looked up at me with her hands over her ears and howled. Her wizened face reminded me of Edvard Munch's painting *The Scream* – she was an anguished figure on the undulating bridge that looked like the hear-no-evil monkey.

The little pet shop on Wharf Street once held an irate baby Woo in a shipping crate. Emily had peered at her once and quickly departed. Woo must have been incensed to have come so far, only to be abandoned by the very creature who had summoned her.

For Emily to have exchanged a precious griffon pup for a monkey, there would have had to been a powerful incentive.

As if in answer, Emily described how she and Woo met.

"Woo took my hand through the bars of her cage. It was the sweetest monkey's paw – a small brown leaf of trust that broke the spell of resistance that my brain had thrown against my wanting. The proprietress let her out and she swung up and clasped my neck with her long arms. She sniffed my neck, squirmed onto my shoulder and began to groom my hair.

That's how she became my 'chip', as I often referred to her, perched. I paraded her in defiance, deliberately invoking the wrath of my sisters and all 'good society'.

"You like to push society's limits."

"Woo and I had a secret."

"I can only imagine," I said.

I felt Emily's memories and caught the nuances that could only be known from personal hindsight. I felt the tugs of all her wantings. I felt the pinch of her corsets and the weight of her long skirts. I knew the discomfort of perching on the edge of chairs; primness was not an attitude it was a physical demand of balance and intakes of breath. I saw Emily sitting at a window, wooing the moon, wiping her sadness into a scented handkerchief. Her young face looked up and made a cameo framed by a windbreak of stars.

I saw a succession of Woo events as the little monkey ate from a vase of sweetheart roses sent by a man she deemed ill-suited for Emily, and watched as she turned the uneaten petals into flying potpourri. I saw Woo hopping up and down with a letter from Martyn in her teeth, knocking Emily's copy of *The Life Everlasting* to the floor in a loud thud. I watched as Woo placed the little ivory elephant in Emily's purse, and another occasion when she swept a black candlestick telephone off the table when it rang with an important call. I saw Emily ignoring Woo's antics, lost in right-brain paint. I saw a familiar Woo in a full-blown hopping tantrum, tearing her blue-flowered dress. I saw Emily preoccupied with art, beyond the call of telephones and letters.

Woo is a connector of dots, leaping from one thing to another to get things noticed.

She is a force to be reckoned with. She is a conundrum: benign *and* threatening, cute and fiendish. One minute I adore her, a heartbeat later, I want to wring her neck. Not that that would do any good. It's me who is becoming unstable. We are a team of three, but there is an imbalance of power. I am calmer when Emily takes a nap.

In a desperate moment, I retrieved Marmie from the back seat while I straightened the mess Woo had made, and asked my old toy to get me home, but it was a small-sized wish. I tucked her into my pocket like old times, and felt somewhat protected. I looked for Woo in the trees and recognized instead, the shadow of Marmie 2. "I haven't seen you in ages," I said. "Can you get me home?"

"Of course," came the answer, "I wondered when you would call me."

I hadn't see Woo for an hour. I figured she was probably off in middle-earth somewhere, brewing a cauldron of love potion number ten. Maybe she was back in her heaven dining on kippers and lettuce, and raisins and wiggity-grubs.

In my intermittent dreams I had a distinct image of Mother Emily, mending a rip down one entire side-seam of a miniature blue-flowered dress. Her eyes were sore from working under a dim lamp. She finished, tidied her sewing basket, and locked it in a cupboard. The key was hidden from monkey fingers.

I had the ability to watch as a remote viewer as well as from inside Emily's mind. I examined her in profile in old age: her blowsy frock, her scowling expression, the set of her wide jaw and frowsy chin, and her iconic hairnet. I imagined Emily with typewriter, awkwardly clacking out her books, hunched over the keys, unwell in her hospital bed, bashing one letter at a time with an index finger.

I wished the maiden Emily would return, but in her passenger seat naps she was the crone, 'Saint Emily of Monkeys' who snored across from me, sending me her hospital fever-dreams.

The sight was dreadful. I wrote my own observations at the next pit stop: 'If Emily was a painting, I would give it the title: 'A Frog Types at Midnight'. Why had this lovely woman given way to gravity and dignity, and passed off her attention for exquisite detail to the beauty of landscape and ignored herself?' It seemed as though Emily deliberately reverted to an outer ugliness to match the inner self-image that she had nurtured for years.

I felt her weight and her urge to smoke. Ugh.

Still I couldn't blame her; Emily was in denial of her creative power, extremely self-critical and always ready to pounce. I guessed that to be proved right, Emily had to look accordingly slovenly. She was always testing the wind for criticism. Like her art, and in spite of her grotesque appearance, Emily dared onlookers to accept or reject her for good reason. Otherwise, her art suffered. Her heart suffered too.

I dialled Jon's number from the service station restroom. He answered on the first ring.

"Jon, I have to talk quickly. Emily and Woo are in the car. Something weird is going on. I didn't notice it till after we left. Perhaps I couldn't.

Emily is presenting two distinct personas. When Woo is asleep, she dithers like a schoolgirl. She is confident and bossy again during Woo's waking hours. They are scaring me.

What's worse, I find myself inside Emily's head, experiencing her memories as my own."

"That's bad," Jon said.

"Emily's form fluctuates from opaque to transparent. When she flickers like a candle, she calls for Woo and fidgets till she comes back. The presence of Woo stabilizes her, for me it's the opposite."

"I think your mission is a done," Jon said, using Emily's phrase.

I reminded him that we had made no contingency for such a thing.

"Make it now," Jon said. "Make it *right* now."

"And Jon, Marmie 2 is here."

"Right now," he repeated. "Do as you're told for once."

I heard my voice say, "Don't tell me what to do. Leave me alone. I don't want you to bother me anymore." Then, I hung up and was violently sick in the sink.

Woo Woo   VERONICA KNOX

I wonder who went with me
in the dream caravan?
I do not remember,
but I was not alone.

~ Emily Carr ~
Hundreds and Thousands

Bridge Over Troubled Ether

he car's interior overhead light was inadequate. My eyes squinted at my journal page. The handwriting I saw was a stranger's. I scribbled more thoughts in my determined travelogue: *It felt like the car was a great beast, heavy as an elephant, that lumbered over the California state line. It's 3 am, I'm running on nerve power – low octane.*

Being near Emily was starting to feel like gambling in a casino that pumped false daylight under my skin. I couldn't sleep. I couldn't forgo sleep. My thinking was erratic. I was awakened by the moon. I needed to stop moving.

"I have the jitters," I announced, "I could have an accident."

"You're picking up on Martyn, I can feel it too."

"Sorry?"

"Martyn has the wedding jitters."

"Emily, no kidding, I'm exhausted. I have to rest."

I saw Emily flinch at my accident remark, and paranoia reared its head. Did Emily want me to die? Was that her plan? Did she want to take over my body like a hermit crab? Would Martyn then covet Jon's? How could I warn him? And then, by remote viewing I could see another me, irrational as a sheet of distraught paper, writing a dear Jon letter. I willed my ka to crumple it up and throw it into a phantom fire. It flashed into a green flame and smelled worse than one of Emily's cigars.

I had to resort to fantasy to keep my eyes open. I pretended the car was a space shuttle and the dark night was outer space. As long as I was on course, I couldn't get lost.

In sleep, Woo's fur was a restful robin's egg blue. My navigator had vanished into her latest dream. I checked the roadmap, but my night vision failed and it blurred into a Jackson Pollock painting.

Blood sugar, the fear of losing Jon, and sleep deprivation swarmed my aching head. I was hungry and thirsty, but most of all, pushed beyond endurance by a woman who had forgotten my body's limitations and basic requirements. Emily's needs filled the car, her needs were driving the car. Today, Emily scared me. I felt like a possessed chauffeur. She had grown noticeably despondent when we veered off course. She kept sighing and fidgeting with her gloves, repeating. "My brother died near here," every few miles.

I hit speed dial to reach Jon. The number shrilled: *he's not home, he's not home, where is he? He's not home.* I let out a primal scream that woke Woo. She copied me (or was I echoing her?) Screams filled the car and Woo's fur turned electric blue with green

WooWoo VERONICA KNOX

sparks. Then, she did a surprising thing. She threw my phone out the window.

I pulled over and searched, but the night had absorbed it. My link to sanity and home was gone.

I sat down on the side of the road with my food hamper and Aloysius, and invited Emily to join me. Woo tagged along looking wary, and all three of us had a heart-to-heartless conversation. My lunch box contained the diet of insomniacs, bottled water, potato chips, and candy bars. I tore off a bottle cap and drank glorious H2O like a dehydrated woman in an oasis. Woo tapped me gingerly on my cheek and opened her hand. On her palm were two sleeping pills.

"Sure you don't want me to take the whole bottle?" I asked. Woo's answering squawk could have meant *yes please, no way,* or *it's about bloody time.*

Emily shimmered like a mirage in a desert. I could see through her to the forest streaming behind. It reminded me of her painted landscapes.

It was night but the heat was unbearable. I think it was the internal heat of Emily's menopause. She was fluctuating from age-to-age now and I had kidded her that she was suffering from man-o-pause. She had laughed, but that was on our first day when we were still in Canada, and making a ghost-run seemed like a lark.

Now, I saw the words as if they were written in chalk on the blackboard of space, my former windshield, where I saw the letters reshuffle to form *pause* and *paws* and *omen.* The spellings came fast, tripping over each other, the way Jon and I played word tag, but our human love games were a thing of the past.

I remembered that I missed Jon. I missed Jenner

and Dolly and Luke. I missed being loved, and I missed being called darling.

I wanted to be home with Canadian rain beating against my bedroom window, phone disconnected, covers pulled up with Dolly and Luke pretending to be one creature with two heads. I craved hot milk and honey, and a wee sedative to cut my anxiety into a flat line of dreaming nothing at all. I craved a color I could sleep in for forty-eight hours.

I pleaded to the stars for aid and collapsed, crying into the teddy-bear of some long-dead child. Rocking it, trying to remember how to breath.

Woo brought me Emily's untouched hot chocolate, and I felt the taste of it revive me a little. Then I heard a faint song coming from the ditch. *It had to be you,* it quavered, and I crawled to it calling: "Jon I'm over here." The tiny box chirruped the lyrics to a lost melody. Jon had changed my ringtone for the trip – an homage to the song from our first date.

I scrambled for the dying notes of my only lifeline. The phone felt warm like an injured bird. It flapped a final text message from Jon that read: *As you wish. I won't bother you anymore.*

Me, the bear, and the phone, curled into a foetal position right there in the grass. I heard Emily crying into her handkerchief. Woo stroked my hair, and everything went black.

"Ma'am, are you okay?"

I heard the syllables 'woo woo' echo in my head. I was trying to speak. "Who? Who?" A light flashed across my eyes and swooped once around the inside of the car.

It was an immaculately dressed police officer.

"Just checking ma'am. You need to move your car. There's sort of a rest stop a mile or two up ahead."

"Sort of?"

"It's a cemetery. If you don't mind that sort of place. Spooks some folks."

"Very funny," I said.

"Ma'am?"

I tried my own joke to test his wit. "A *final* resting place then?" I quipped, but he didn't laugh. His eyes showed trained concern, with no sense of humor. *A robot cop,* I thought, and smiled.

"Ma'am?"

"Nothing, Sorry officer. I had to sleep for a bit. I'll be on my way."

"Wait, I have coffee," he said, "do you have a cup?"

I rummaged for the paper cup and drained the last few drops of chocolate flavored water as he returned with a thermos.

"You're not like the average American police officer, I mean state trooper – the ones we foreigners are warned about. You are creatures of legend, you know."

"This is California, ma'am. We're not so uptight."

I was quick to clarify, "I wasn't complaining."

"Canadians don't as a rule."

"Touché," I said.

"Ma'am?"

"To stereotypes," I said, lifting the paper cup in a weak toast and drank the gift of instant consciousness in one swig.

"That's nice perfume you're wearing."

It was my turn to question the obvious. "Perfume?"

"It's lavender, right? Reminds me of my grandma."

"Right on ... er the money," I continued."I'm awake enough to drive now. A couple of miles ahead you say?"

"Less than five minutes."

"Thanks for the coffee."

"You take care now. Drive safe."

I watched officer robot do a U turn in my rear view mirror and head back the way I'd come, and for a wild minute I wanted to follow. I wanted home and Jon's sharp mind, and Jenner's amber eyes, and the heft of my living apartment key. Somewhere north of here, I thought, I might still have a life.

"Very droll," Emily said. "Thanks for rubbing it in."

Emily waved her handkerchief to fan me. It was the source of the lavender. "That's my girl," she said, and I felt leveled by a low blow.

"I am not anybody's girl," I snapped, "and stay out of my head!"

Emily was tracing her finger over the roadmap. "We have to turn onto Route..."

"Emily, that nap wasn't enough. I'm going to have a proper rest." With those Spartan words, I shut off my phone and shoved it into the glove compartment.

"Two miles ahead," Emily said, as Woo danced a shell-pink jig on Emily's head rest. "Don't worry I have all the time in the world."

We pulled into the Marin County Cemetery where I found a grove of shade trees, and parked under a sun about to wake.

Woo Woo VERONICA KNOX

I rolled down the windows and fixed a makeshift bed in the back seat. Aloysius made a hard pillow. I checked my passengers before I pressed play on my MP3 player.

It was no big surprise that the scene in front of me resembled a surreal painting. A magenta Woo frolicked in the redwoods leaping from branch to branch leaving strobe lights of hot pink and gold. Emily had set up an easel to paint. A large melted pocket watch had been casually draped over a branch and revealed that it was now six o-clock.

My silver car transformed into a box. Emily's voice rang out to rattle me: "It's a box-Carr" and trailed off into a laugh. I recalled the written words of Emily's memoirs: *There it sat, grey and lumbering like an elephant by the roadside.*

My car grazed in a grove of cedar, its passenger door flung open like a giant elephant's ear. A campsite sprawled before it as a hobo's picnic. Emily glanced over at me; she was in her element. "Sweet dreams," she called out, and turned back to her paints.

The thoughts *rest in peace* ran through my mind and Emily heard me. She delivered a last comment. "You're going to be just fine!" she shouted. This time it was her voice inside my head.

I pretended I was five. I cuddled Marmie under my chin, and turned up the volume of my audio book. The gentle strains of Harry Potter's opening theme music announced *Harry Potter and the Philosopher's Stone,* and Stephen Fry's voice led me into an English countryside where I dreamed it rained hard against the stained-glass windows of Hogwarts castle.

I smelled a Thanksgiving dinner, laid on a several banquet tables, each of them two miles long.

Levitating chandeliers lit the hall and ghosts floated above the tables. A blonde teenage boy, carrying a teddy-bear, offered me a plate of mile-high, stuffed Yorkshire pudding, and winked. He was wearing the black graduation robe of an Oxford don and a Gryffindor scarf.

I heard Emily and Woo discussing me. "Is she sleeping?" Emily asked.

Woo's small high voice was how I imagined piglet's from *Winnie the Pooh* when he had been breathless with excitement: "What color shall we paint her dream?" she said, and added: "I think blue is best."

"It depends which shade of blue," Emily said.

The word blue overwhelmed me. I stared into a pair of Aegean blue eyes, and then I was in Victoria, back in the Hill House garden on Simcoe Street, dizzy from happiness. The air was heavy with the intoxicating scent of sweet peas and I was a child amongst a towering forest of hollyhock trees. My daisy parasol lay where it had fallen, in the center of a fairy circle that formed a pale sage-green island in a clearing of bright spring moss. I heard the sound of tiny disappearing hooves from the other side of a thicket of mauve rocket.

My fairy horse galloped between the daffodils and fallen berries, and I called out for my invisible boy: *Jon where are you?* I heard my name called carried by a soft breeze: *Scottieeeeeeeeee,* but Jon turned into a seagull, and I had to watch helplessly as he flew out over the tadpole pond and into the cumulus mountains of the sky.

I woke and stretched my legs outside, propped Marmie in her place of honour on the dashboard with her arms clasping my phone, sipped some cold coffee, and started the car. The road was deserted. I needed to phone Drummie... or someone. Someone I had hurt. The disturbances were multiplying. I was absorbing Emily's memories and latent fears. I felt them as my own conscience, breathing in the heady perfumes of childhood or choking on cloying courtship, suffocating for the fresh air of spinsterhood. I was jumping out of my skin, staring at the silent phone.

I confused an oncoming vehicle's horn with an incoming call. My autopilot swerved the car onto the grass verge to avoid a head-on collision. Neither Emily nor Woo registered fear and the two of them appeared well and more solid the more I withered.

Emily's old fears jostled for attention and tapped an SOS on the inside of my skull, hammering out a three painkiller headache accompanied by dark-angel advice. A gold Marmie 2 on one shoulder and a silver Woo on the other, debated the pros and cons of cremation or burial without a coffin, trying to rationalize me down from Emily's old ledge.

Death was consuming all the energy around me. My phone battery had died. I swooned and dreamed I was home, looking out my window. I waved to Jon and Jenner, who were standing in St. Ann's under the same tree that had captured Woo the night we posted Emily's letter. I could see the sign on the gate: 'St. Ann's Academy' with Ann spelled plain without the 'e'.

Monkey Busy-ness

*E*mily was stalling. "My brother Dick died near here, when I was away at school," she recited, as if hypnotized. "I'd better go look for him," she said, and got out of the car.

Emily lifted her head to listen as a male voice shouted: "catch me up". She stared blankly at the tall cemetery gates for a moment before turning away. I watched her wander off and melt into a copse of evergreens.

Woo clambered up the gate's lock and chains and cleared the spikes at the top in one leap. She skipped out of sight in hot pursuit of Martyn, and I paled, left alone in the semi-darkness, facing another ghostly encounter.

I pushed gently on the wrought iron, expecting resistance, but the chains dropped away in a slither of steel pearls and the gate squealed open. There was no trace of Emily.

I took Marmie out of my coat pocket. My flashlight pen showed me her earring was still intact, before its beam flickered and died. I gripped her tightly, made a wish, and called for Marmie 2. Immediately

I saw her distinct white form glide over the trees like the passing shadow of a night owl.

Woo's answering shriek was distorted – buffeted by the wind. I heard Emily calling Woo from far away. I should give them all some privacy, I thought, and hung back – a coward for confrontation.

Then I heard Emily laughing and a man's voice calling my name.

"Scottie, where are you?"

My knees were ice, but I replied in a casual singsong voice like a reluctant child answering its mother: "Coming," and headed towards the tryst – ahead and to the right, in the golden trees that now looked like they were on fire. The path was steep, and I ignored the grave markers and statues of white angels, and the row of mausoleums like vacation houses for the dearly departed that lined the way to the happy voices.

It was like the reports I'd heard of near death experiences. I approached a loving white light and the objects either side of me blurred into a tunnel. I sleepwalked towards a feeling of great affection. I felt safe. A transparent Woo, dressed in white, materialized from the small sun that drew me in. She held out her hand, jumped to my shoulder, placed a sprig of orange blossom in my hair, and chirruped like a bird.

The light dazzled my vision. "Emily are you okay?" I whispered, as I inched forward. "Where are you?"

"Over here," she called back.

Emily stood, resting her head on Martyn's shoulder. His arm was firmly draped around her tiny waist, supporting the radiance which was Emily in youthful splendor, calm and confident. She still wore her navy travelling suit and matching hat.

"Call me Will," Martyn said, as he shook my hand. His handshake was warm and solid, and I relaxed slightly. I felt strangely protected by his presence, but then I realized I was feeling what Emily had felt that day on the platform at Paddington station, in London all those years ago. I wondered what Scottie would be feeling, but I didn't have to wonder for long.

I gawped for an age, speechless, and started to laugh uncontrollably.

"Sorry I'm a bit hysterical," I explained.

"You're allowed," Martyn said.

William Paddon was a tall broad-shouldered shape eclipsed by the glowing light behind him.

"Sorry, you'll always be Martyn to me, if that's okay."

"Anything for a girl who can frighten my Emily. Jon wants you home. Let's go. I made him a promise."

I left them for a while and returned to my car. Blue light clung to my body like a mist of wet sparks. The forest waivered with stripes of light and I assumed Emily was pushing them into animation.

While Emily and Martyn cuddled on a stone bench, I tried my phone and was surprised to get a signal.

Jon answered on the first ring with three words: "Where are you?" and I burst into sobs. "Come ... home," he said slowly, as if talking to a simpleton. "Leave the car there and fly."

"Emily won't fly," I said, and it sounded ridiculous, even in my altered state. What could she be afraid of in her condition? Love conquers fear and apparently death itself, so falling from the sky... and then I remembered, it was me who feared the flight experience. Maybe Emily had been considerate by demanding that we drove.

"Scottie, are you there? Please say something."

"Is déjà vu one of your paranormal specialties?" I managed.

"Talk to me."

"Everything feels familiar. I don't remember me anymore. Tell me something. Who was I? Remind me."

"I love you. Remember that? Scottie?"

"I do." My voice sounded like Emily saying her wedding vows.

"You have a dog named Jenner. He's right here. Speak to him. He's jumping all over the place."

"Why are you calling me Scottie?"

"Come home Scottie. Right now! Please."

I heard my voice say: "I can't marry you, Martyn. It would be wicked and cruel, because I don't love that way. Besides – my work."

"It's me. Jon. Hang work; I can support us. You do love me."

"It's not support; it's not money or love; it's the work itself. And, Martyn, while you are around me, I am not doing my best. Martyn please go away!"

I recognized Emily's words from her book, 'Growing Pains.' I knew, because I recalled the day I wrote them. I remembered them as part of a real conversation. I remembered Emily's body language with her nerves at wits' end, and Martyn's devastated expression, and that he cried. I remembered the horrific guilt. For sure, I never wanted to do that to Jon.

My voice continued to speak. It sounded as if I was shouting under water. "Billy go home. You have to leave me alone. I can't take any more. You're making me ill. I'm so sorry you came so far. Please go away. I need to concentrate on school."

"Scottie that's not you, it's Emily," a stranger's voice said.

The name Scottie woke me up a little. "Jon?" I managed to croak.

"Get in the car and drive away. Call 911. Get your ass on a plane, right now."

"She'll only follow me. I have to see this through to be free. I've promised a ghost. Just like you did, to Click."

"You made a promise to me too," he said.

"Why am I in a sanatorium? I have to go. No phones are allowed in here."

"Jenner is going nuts," the stranger said, "and so am I," and then the line went dead.

Martyn came all the way
from Canada to London
just to see me,
and with him he lugged that great love
he had offered to me.

~ Emily Carr ~
Growing Pains

Cold Feet, Lukewarm Hearts, & Hot Pursuit

he constant flipping from my memories to Emily's, gave me a better understanding of hide-and-seek clues. Approaching a target was considered getting warm, but warmer for me, meant the cooling of passion. My relationship with Jon was somewhere on the moon, and the road begged me to grow up. Emily took me aside and begged me to steel myself against eventual heartache. She said there was no courtship without ownership.

I used to believe that, and was sure I would again. Emily had exchanged her fears about love's great conquest for my eager ones. I wanted no part of an intimate relationship anymore. I felt my enthusiasm for love falter as I watched Emily and Martyn's blossom. Emily and I had effectively changed sides. Same fence; different grass. Emily's was greener now. Mine had become the same brown thatch as her grave.

The cure for a common romance was clearly real

food and plenty of bed rest. My right baby toe hurt like a bugger. I didn't dare take off my shoe in case it wasn't there. Emily's toe had been amputated in London. From far off, I could see Jon getting into his Jeep and Jenner bounding into the back seat. I watched them peel away from the curb on Humboldt Street, and the determined look on Jon's face. I tried yelling "stay there!" but my voice broke like shattered glass, and the pain in my foot reminded me I was not a ghost.

I stopped at a liquor store and bought the smallest bottle of brandy they had, and found a motel where they offered twenty-four hour room service.

"I'm stopping here for a hot meal, a nip of this and a decent nights sleep," I told Martyn. He didn't argue. Woo grabbed the flat bottle and upended it, glugging it back for a few seconds. I grabbed it from her and drank without wiping the lip. I was becoming frantic again, but the fiery drink settled what nerves I had left.

I asked the question I'd been longing to ask. "What! for the love of Hanuman, does Woo still want?" I yelled.

"Ask *her*," Emily snapped, her warm happy eyes narrowing to a cold stare.

Martyn shushed her. "We owe Scottie a rest," he said to Emily. "We're together now. There's no need to hurry."

Emily smiled apologetically, "I haven't been myself, as I'm sure you've noticed. I have no excuses. Some day we will understand I suppose. Right now I need to put things right. I am so very sorry."

"I can relate," I countered.

I looked for Woo, she was curled up on her side clutching Marmie, snoring drunk. Logic told me she was more receptive tipsy, and so I addressed my question to her exposed ear. "Woo, what is your problem?"

There was a slight buzzing in my own ear. I heard a tiny high-pitched voice, and miraculously, Woo articulated her feelings calmly.

I translated for Emily, "Woo is still miffed over some zoo thing," I said. "She felt abandoned and died alone from a broken heart. In Stanley Park, she says."

Emily started to cry. Martyn pretended to be asleep. Woo woke up groggy and came unglued. She began to comfort Emily by giving her my bear. She lugged him from the passenger seat the way a caveman drags his cave-spouse by the hair and ears. I flinched. Aloysius was in no condition to be so manhandled. His left ear came away in Woo's hand, and regular chaos turned to bedlam. Woo's distress dried Emily's tears faster than any ministrations of simian compassion. Martyn snoozed through the whole episode, I think to be tactful. He knew more than he let on. I decided that I liked him for it.

I quickly retrieved the threadbare ear and whispered into it, "don't worry I have a sewing kit in the glove compartment" and put the ear in my purse. Apparently I had gone insane.

For all the trouble Woo had caused, she didn't snore all the way home. I envied her the ability to fall into sleep, deeper than a cat, but then she wasn't sleeping, she was hibernating. Conserving her energy for the big day to come.

I drove with caution, and from time to time caught a glimpse of Emily and Martyn wrapped in each other's arms, sleeping with smiles on their faces. I was the only one awake, so I listened to my audio tape and pretended my car could fly within a cloaking device. I couldn't remember if I was replaying the starship distraction or Harry Potter. All I knew was I was under a spell with a mission to journey north to a planet called Ross Bay.

All that love spilt over me
and I let it spill,
Standing in the middle of the puddle of it;
angry at being drenched
and totally unable to accept
or return it.

~ Emily Carr ~
Hundreds and Thousands
1936

It Was a Trip!

fter we disembarked from the ferry at Swartz Bay, Woo perched on my car like a hood ornament the rest of the way home. Her red dress blew in the wind like a small red flag making us look like a diplomat's vehicle.

Emily's gaze in the mirror, mouthed "thank you." Sometimes she and Martyn were children. Once they were very old, but then they stabilized into the solid dream of their twenties. Backseat lovers who had ducked their monkey chaperone.

I was lost in my own drama. My silent phone made me antsy. I had wanted to hurl it over the rail of the ferry, and when Woo reached for it after a long stare into my soul, I realized she was reading my mind and would have been only too thrilled to comply once more. I believe she also wanted to thank me, and that some small destructive favor would be taken as a pleasure. She had meant no malice and I had been hallucinating for much of the time, under the influence of ethereal laws. I would never make light of metaphysics again.

At one point, when Emily had been napping, Martyn had volunteered some phenomena of his own. "There were times, in the thirties, when the countryside of Marin county moved like a kaleidoscope," he said. "Its colours glowed, illuminated from within, pulsing and singing. It was at those moments I thought of Emily. I knew she was painting and sharing her love with me the only way she could. There were bad times as well, when she was in a panic and I felt drowsy under the medication she'd been given. When you left Victoria, I could feel she was on her way, not as time is reckoned, but by the colour of the sky."

My phone rang with the sinister reverb of a record slowly spinning on a dying turntable. I answered it and spoke with relief. To my surprise, I knew what to say. I needn't bother with diplomacy. There would be the quiet love of friendship in my final goodbye.

After we had crossed the Canadian border with Martyn, Emily's energy left me and I felt wholly myself, but residual doubt persisted. More than anything, I wanted to avert a romantic disaster with Jon. The only permanent way was to stop playing inside a delusion, blissful as it had been for a while.

Love was too much of a gamble. I had been perfectly content living alone, and I would be again. I craved my quiet life. I felt ruined for love. I didn't blame Emily, and my inflated impressions of Woo,

WooWoo VERONICA KNOX

had been a direct result of the hysteria transferred from Emily. I had been playing out the rules of the deceased. No harm had ever been intended. All of us had been sorely tested. I had learned a valuable lesson about perception, and developed a new respect for the human nervous system, but romance had died.

I felt I had been reprieved from the starry-eyed dream that I had been floating in for the last month. I had come to my senses. It was early enough to end with Jon, but now there was the reality of life beyond death to contend with. No doubt I would eventually process it. For now, it gave me indigestion to consider it, and I still had the wedding to endure. No way was I going to sabotage my eventual freedom by breaching a metaphysical contract.

Jon listened. He was so silent I thought he may have hung up. "It's best that we separate," I began. "I love you. I just don't love you enough. After this ordeal I can honestly say I never want a romantic relationship again. Ever. That's final. I will pick up Jenner on Monday. If you love me, please don't try to talk me out of this. I have to be alone for a while. Please understand. I am so sorry."

The Secret Garden

The graveyard 'garden' was waiting, dappled in supernatural light. Globes of tea-lights hung from the trees like giant fireflies. The night sky hung in an arc of dusty light connecting Victoria to San Diego in a rainbow of ethereal fog. Tiny, white fairy-horses the size of cats, galloped amongst the stone markers leaving a wake of effervescent energy.

The loud caw of a Raven split the silence, bedazzled by the shiny rings that Woo flaunted so brazenly under its beak. She had camouflaged herself into crow colors, stealing from the yellow beak and blue-black feathers. Woo looked like she was wearing a bee costume, and as soon as she heard my thought, she danced a quick spiral, and presented herself in her best red dress. My earrings glittered on her wrist as bangle bracelets. It was her turn to screech her own victory crow in my direction.

The blackbird gave a last protest swoop, dive bombed low over the amethyst tiara in Emily's hair and flew into the moon. I saw its dark feathers flash into a lime green parrot and then a white cockatoo that burst in a firework of platinum sparks. "Sally is a Sally," echoed a bird's voice, and Emily's up-turned face gasped with the innocent delight of a child.

"Birds of Paradise," I commented, and Emily beamed. Her form flickered like a lantern, and I thought she might actually dematerialize from happiness.

Emily's gown was hour-glass mauve. I watched her silhouetted against the moonlight and followed her gaze. At first I saw nothing, but then I could see the vision which captivated her attention: it was a growing totem pole shimmering in shades of silver. Its inhabitants were carved deep. It had a lion rampant base to honor Queen V, and as it rose higher, it morphed into dogs and cats and a parrot with its wings extended to form the traditional cross shape. A monkey came last with a rat on top of its head. Emily was weeping.

"IMP! Scallywag!" came Emily's voice, but laughter betrayed her anger. Woo was trying to catch the horses, pelting them with pinecones. Martyn ignored the whole thing. His eyes never left his bride-to-be.

The most beautiful things fell apart...
The boy and the horses were gone.

~ Emily Carr ~
The Book of Small

Something Borrowed;
Someone Blue

The wisdom of making Woo the ring bearer had not been thought through. Her magic was overestimated, her simian nature had been sorely underrated.

Emily's preferred cathedral was unavailable. The formal garden of the Ross Bay Cemetery had to stand in for the natural columns of divine redwood and cedar she preferred. She had wanted the fingers of god-light to spill through the orange spars and the sound of wild hawks and howling wolves. She wanted the colours of autumn striped with turquoise and emerald. She wanted the sacred grove of Drummie's wedding chapel watched over by a vine named Isabella. She wanted all of that, and she wasn't one to settle.

'Vincent's' wedding gift was a shimmering canopy of starry night embroidered with a full, lemon moon that rose, refracted under moving ripples of water. He had pulled an empty brush over the navy-blue firmament while the paint was wet. Fingers of lilac moonlight wavered into a blur of striped wallpaper. Underneath it, Emily stood radiant next to her tall bridegroom. They held hands between two growing pillars of transparent oak. The lowest branches had bent low, clasping each-to-each in an arch that framed them like a portal.

The evening was like a day viewed through lavender-tinted glasses, the expensive ones that cost more than a bridal gown in 1871, the year Emily displaced the molecules of a snowstorm and stirred the feminine calm of 44 Carr Street off Birdcage Walk, into a frenzy of befuddled energy.

It had taken four years for William Paddon to catch *her* up.

A midnight wind rattled the holly hedge as Woo scarpered off with opposable-thumb perversity, her eyes glittering bright as the diamond solitaire and gold band clutched in her brown fingers.

Miss W was showing off. Her red dress could be seen from below like the last autumn leaf caught in the branches. She whooped her way to a grey squirrel, gloating over her treasure, and their over-excited exchange of chatter-speak scared the invited birds: doves, budgies, canaries, parrots and cockatoos, rose in one great flapping of agitation. Wings of ivory and azure, marigold and crimson, fluttered in a cloud of raked stars.

The commotion shocked a lone peacock's tail into glory. The eyes on the tip of each feather scanned the garden of white gravestones and fanned the monkey's private conversation into a piercing brown shriek that made Emily laugh in a loud guffaw. She yelled, "Woo!" and waved her bouquet of orange blossoms like a cheerleader at the red balloon drifting towards the lilac sky. "Get down here!"

The nimble red dress paused for a moment, looked down at Emily, and replied, cheekily: *I'm busy right now!* They were like an old married couple, but the red dress reluctantly returned to earth in a casual acrobatic trapeze as it swung in a low arc, and landed defiantly. Emily held out her hand.

Woo approached in a slow waddle and meekly handed over the jewels, but firmly claimed the pillow that once bore them towards the makeshift altar. When she was rebuked, she bared her teeth in monkey bravado and delivered a lecture of simian profanity befitting a disheveled lady in a torn red party frock.

Scold-for-scold, Emily and Woo were a match made in heaven, which is ironic, because it's been over sixty years since they both passed on.

My emotions were in battle mode. I was ecstatic for Emily and in mourning at the same time, but I was not alone. Emily flashed me a silent message that said it was okay to be blissfully happy and freaked-out at the same time because lovers exist on a different planet. Martyn turned and winked a secret that made me want to cry.

Now I know for sure, that being in love really is a form of insanity, and one must embrace the madness in order to defy the odds against being a ship passed in the night. True love is a many-layered thing that defies time and death.

Woo settled on the top of a bench tomb, laid her head on her silk pillow, and closed her eyes pretending she wasn't there. A generous shaft of moonlight kept her hypnotized and quiet.

The cemetery returned to the aura of a church as the stars continued to celebrate a less-traditional match under deepening ever greens and forever blues turned to indigo. The ceremony was simple; a preacher and vows were unnecessary for a wedding larger than life.

The tune *Oh Promise Me* played in my head. Jon had promised Click. I had promised Emily. Martyn and Emily had just made a new promise to each other: *to love, though death tries to part us*. I stood on a lavender island of manicured grass, and held onto one clear thought, that thankfully this evening would be a thing of the past by daybreak.

Then by and by I had a sweetheart.
He wanted me to love him and I couldn't,
but one day I almost did.

~ Emily Carr ~
Growing Pains

A Double Wedding Not

It takes two to complete a wedding vow, two to have a conversation, and two to tango. The couple that had been Jon and I were no more, I had decided for the two of us.

It was pitch moonlight, the ceremony was over. The guests had retreated to their woodlands and skies. All but Woo, and a pair of white horses, wings folded, wearing white plumes, hitched to the dream of a carriage as Emily and her Martyn were bound together as husband and wife.

The word wife felt foreign. I would never be one.

I heard a thought serenaded by the mew of a seagull as I closed my eyes: *My dreams are gathered here, together, to unite this man and this woman, and that man and that woman, in theoretical matrimony.*

If I ever have the urge to keep a diary for recording my most intimate secrets, which I won't, I would preface the baring of my soul with these three words: destroy before reading.

The horses were full-size and stunning. Moonlight had turned their coats to pale blue. Woo had become a purple lantern shape hanging from a high branch, staring off into the horizon like the lookout of a tall ship. I wondered if she was peering into the past or the future, and if it was for better or worse.

I have always cried at weddings and never knew why. I've never been sentimental over gush-love. Until now.

Martyn on the platform at Euston Station
was like a bit of British Columbia,
big strong and handsome.

~ Emily Carr ~
Growing Pains

The Honeymoon Sweet

he arc of Emily's orange blossom bouquet soared in slow motion towards me, but the swift arm of Woo snatched it from the air, inches from my face. Monkey chuckling echoed from somewhere behind me. I had not been present enough to even attempt to catch it.

Woo scooted off with her prize and my eyes followed her. The shadows parted and Jon stood there with Jenner, like a silvered sentinel at the back of the church grove – the ghost of love's future, with a fresh bouquet of white sweetheart roses.

He held the flowers out to me with that devastating smile of his. Woo dropped Emily's bouquet, reached up to Jon's and accepted them. She ran back to me, delivering them with a delighted chirp.

I plucked the head from a delicate blossom and gave it to Woo. She looked at it curiously and I watched it turn deep red. When Woo was satisfied with the colour, she munched the fragrant petals in ecstasy.

Later, I dubbed Jon my Shining 'Night' in silver

amour. My sourpuss expression evaporated as the dawn chorus sang Emily and Martyn into an invisible horse-drawn limo. I didn't see them go, but I assumed they disappeared to the happily hereafter.

Woo waited, jumping up and down excitedly, eager to join the delighted couple. The matchmaker from Java was ever-determined to tie a just-married sign on her mission.

Emily had gotten her peacock, as well as several screech owls that had tried to out-screech Woo, with no success. It had been the eeriest, most apropos choir for a graveyard at midnight.

Was it real? I felt a sharp pinch on my leg and looked down into a monkey grimace that crinkled Woo's eyes closed. She looked blissful, as if she were making a wish. She opened her eyes, chortled, and I saw her wink as she blew out one of the tea lights to make her wish official. I watched her skip towards the sea whooping with some private joke of hers, but she turned back at the edge of Dallas Road, the farthest boundary of the cemetery, as if she could go no further. She loped back towards us still hooting with excitement.

Jon had crossed the space between us and it stunned me momentarily to be the recipient of such intimacy again. I dropped my bouquet and Woo grabbed it, and chattered over the white roses until all of them had turned red.

Jenner licked my hand, and Woo gave him the kind of look only a monkey guarding an armful of juicy roses could express.

"Come here you big lug," I said to Jon, to coin a shameless phrase.

"Gull," Jon corrected. "Backwards for lug."

"Morning Seagull," I said.

"Not any more, I'm not."

"I don't und..."

"The *mourning* is finally over," Jon said.

I was overtired and nervous as a bride. "One little 'u' and the world changes," I said, and apologized for being so corny.

"You don't know from corny," Jon said. "It had to be u," he said slyly, and his deep, Aegean Blue, twinkling come-to-bed eyes, framed in thick lashes, musk to die for, completely cheeky, utterly charming, lanky as a pop star, swirled together in a blur of impressionist colors and kissed me with his sensuous mouth.

We emerged on Fairfield Road. It started to rain silver stars. Jon's watch said it was six o-clock. "Race you to the Eggs Benedict," I said.

Then, by and by I had a sweetheart.
He wanted me to love him and I couldn't,
but one day I almost did.

~ Emily Carr ~
Growing Pains

Happy Ever Afterlife

oo shrieked her last wild kingdom incantation. The wedding breakfast called. Woo knew where to go and we followed her as she intended – towards mayhem and sugar. Eggs Benedict was sadly a few hours away.

Woo led Jon and I to the nearest Tim Hortons where we snagged the best table by the window. Not surprisingly, we had the place to ourselves, although a straggle of cars already crept past the takeout window. The dawn was still in its aurora borealis phase.

We toasted the missing happy couple with morning's finest champagne – strong java. Still feeling nervous and corny, we raised our donuts and clinked them soundlessly together. The gentle impact of Jon's Boston Cream and my classic jam-filled Bismark dusted with powdered sugar made a white puff like a small cloud. Jon still looked ashen. He put down his donut, un-tasted. I could tell there was a lot he needed to say.

I joked us into a familiar place. "It's just as well that Emily chose not to wear white," I said to ease the tension, "white can make a person look like death warmed up."

"Not quite the look Emily was going for," Jon said.

"It wasn't the experience I was going for either," I said.

Jon toyed with his stir stick. "You couldn't have known."

"I am so sorry," I said. "Why did you send me that text?"

"What text?"

"The one that said you wouldn't bother me any more."

"No way. Not me. I never sent you a text like that. I remember that I kept getting the same wrong number while I was waiting to hear from you, and when it rang again, I said politely, "I wish you wouldn't bother me anymore."

"The heart hears what it needs to hear."

Jon smiled in a wan imitation of Jay Gatsby, and pushed his plate towards me. "Shut up and take the first bite," he said. "It's five stars."

The aroma of fresh-brewed coffee kept us conscious and stirred a transparent Woo into a caffeine frenzy as she explored the display trays of donuts, leaping from shelf to shelf. Biting one and tossing it on the floor, beguiled by frosting and sprinkles. Each merited a taste and no more, till she experienced the monkey-sized 'Timbits'. Jon and I watched Woo change into a pattern of bright colored specks.

"There's Emily's hundreds and thousands," I said.

We watched Woo gather an armload of assorted flavours and retreat to a corner to mutter over her hoard, discreetly giving us our privacy while she plucked jewel-like raisins, chocolate chips, and nuts from a sunrise muffin the size of her brain.

"I think Woo must have caffeine in her blood," I said. "Not to mention cream and jam and chocolate frosting."

"I'd say Woo is a tad over the limit," Jon agreed.

I took Jon's hand. "You look white as a ghost," I said, to break the ice that had started to form again. Jon looked shaken and I encouraged him to tell his side of the story. "I saw you and Jenner get in your car," I began. "What happened after that?"

"Did you? I hit the road pretty fast with Jenner. I was in a panic. We got as far as the ferry... er... *terminal*. God, I hate that word, now. I was talking with you, and my phone battery died. The line of cars started to move and so I turned the ignition. Nothing. The car had died too. Someone helped me push it to the side, and a mechanic was summoned by a ferry worker. His verdict was worse than a dead battery. There was nothing to be done but call for a tow.

A truck arrived and when it turned the car towards Victoria, the engine started by itself. The key was in my pocket, and Jenner was barking like a maniac at the car. I got a lecture for leaving a key in the ignition and had to pay the guy sixty bucks for his pains.

I tested my theory. I drove past Sydney, pulled into a service station and turned back towards the ferry. The car stalled. There was no juice. I got help pushing it around to face the city again, and it started. I drove home, to your place.

Dolly and Luke were shredding the drapes and had knocked over every ornament, except Emily's elephant, which was sitting by itself in the center of the coffee table. The answer machine was off, its plug pulled out. Kitty litter had been raked out of the box. Both cats were acting like a couple of, dare I say, monkeys. Jenner tried to herd them into a corner. They swore at him and he retreated behind me.

Against all the rules for restoring calm, I yelled, *cut it out right now*, and they did. They became their old selves and sidled up to Jenner, purring. Clearing up the mess gave me something to do. It's fairly tidy now, but there wasn't much I could do about the curtains.

When I took Jenner for his midnight pee across the street, I looked up at your apartment window. You were there and I saw you wave at us. I rushed up the stairs to find two cats sleeping, but no you. So I sat down and did something I actually abhor."

Jon looked embarrassed. "What?" I blurted out.

Jon took a deep breath. "I conducted a séance... I invoked the dead."

I almost laughed, but Jon's face was serious. "But, that's a normal part of your investigations isn't it?"

"No. Never. That is someone else's thing. Whenever I make personal contact I let the ghost come to me. I just wait and listen. This time I acted like a ditzy medium and called the only person I could think of. I channelled Martyn."

"How? What did you say?"

Jon tried to remember. "Something inanely standard like: *William Paddon. Are you there? If you can hear me, I need you to help a woman named Scottie headed your way. She's a friend of Emily's and she needs to come home. I love her. It's a matter of love and death.*"

"Always the wise guy," I said.

"I do my best."

I leaned over and stole a long kiss. "That's one of the things you do best," I said.

"Wait, there's more. My phone had gone awol (evidently at Woo's command) It turned up at your place," he said. "The morning you left, I had wanted to surprise you holding Aloysius and a picnic basket, leaning on your car."

"With a rose in your teeth?"

"How did you guess? I even snipped off all the thorns so neither of us would shed blood. I figured we were already wounded enough. I set my alarm, but it didn't go off. When I woke up, the food hamper was in the kitchen, but the bear was gone. And by the way, Trudi didn't leave that message, Woo did. Emily told me so before she and Martyn left."

Jon stooped down and gave me the sweetest kiss, tender, fraught as a passionate love letter.

Brewing coffee scented our conversation which centered on not heading to either of our apartments.

"My bag is still in my car," I said, and the word 'Carr' hit us both.

Jon squeezed my sky-blue shoulder."Which *car* shall we take?" he countered.

"I think yours. Mine may need to be exorcised."

"That reminds me. Jenner needs to be exercised. We better go."

We pooled our resources. Between us we had enough credit for a dog-friendly motel and new toothbrushes. Later on we would discuss details.

Woo, the jungle sprite, had vanished. The last of her kind, I guessed.

When we reached my car, Emily's bridal bouquet shimmered on my driver's seat, lit from within like a lantern, and as I reached for it, it evaporated and exposed Marmie, her arms wrapped around my missing Salvador Dali watch.

He was different from other boys,
you did not have to see him,
That was why I liked him so.

~ Emily Carr ~
The Book of Small

Heaven Forefend

"Happy first anniversary," Jon and I said, addressing the tablet in the bright green grass with raised thermos cups of strong Orange Pekoe. It was pouring cats and dogs, but I searched the Ross Bay Cemetery's trees for a single monkey in a dry red dress. Woo still had my earrings.

I pointed at the grave. "They aren't down there," I said through the rain, as I held on tight to my umbrella, in case a monkey's paw grabbed it. It was my favorite, imprinted with Van Gogh's *Starry Night*, and it brought back memories of the year before, when the painted sky had sanctified the union of Emily and Martyn with its swooning colors and striated moonbeams.

"But, it's their last known whereabouts, ergo, a symbolic place to offer one's respect," Jon said.

I tossed back my warm tea like a shot of whisky and squeezed Jon's arm. Tea and rain, Jon and Jenner. Dolly and Luke waiting at home. Our new home with its garden: I couldn't wish for more.

"To Mr. and Mrs. Paddon," I declared, and I swear I heard a subdued woo woo victory cheer from the sodden tree line. "Woo! Woo! Woo!" I mimicked with the accompanying celebratory gesture of a cranking fist circling my ear.

Jon shouted: "To the art of marriage!" and tipped the last drops of his tea over the bronzed name, Emily Carr, as a libation. It splashed, made a miniature brown puddle, and was quickly diluted by the downpour.

A first anniversary is paper and carnations... we gave them a copy of Jon's new book on reincarnation and figured we had it covered. The deluge would claim it, turn it to pulp, and return it to nature as a liquid tree. Reincarnation indeed. We left Woo her favorite food.

"Hey, you wanna grab a bite?" Jon asked, with a twinkle in his eye.

"Stuffed Yorkie!" I twinkled back, with enthusiasm.

Jon flashed me one of his devastating grins. "Race you across the street!"

"Last one there is a rotten Chicken Korma," I shouted.

Behind us lay a drenched patch of happiness, Jon's book, a head of lettuce, and a bridal bouquet with a card that read:

to Emily and Martyn
~ R.I.P ~
Rest In Perpetuity

P.S. the lettuce is for Woo

> *I wonder will we ever*
> *consciously look back*
> *and see the plan of things,*
> *the reason for this and that*
> *and the good of it?*
>
> ~ Emily Carr ~
> *Hundreds and Thousands*

After the Math

Of course, given the intrepid reporters that Jon and I were, we continued to press deeper for details. The serenity we *dipped* into revealed some surprises. In other words, we did the math.

Something big is going to go down in 2046. On March 2nd. Jon will still officially be seventy-four, the same age as Emily when she passed over, and the 100th anniversary of the death of a monkey named, Woo.

During the trip south to San Diego, we had both experienced nausea or stomach cramps when phoning each other – Woo's version of the 'Pavlov's Dog' negative reinforcement effect. Each attempted call was a crossed wire or an imaginary conversation that Woo played in our minds. She took no chances; her first loyalty was to Emily.

Here are a few of the serendipitous dots we connected:

Emily was born in 1871 – Jon was born one-hundred-years later, in 1971. Emily's mother died in

1886 when she was fifteen; she was seventeen when her father died. I was fifteen when my father died and seventeen when my mother died. In 1946, Woo passed away at the age of fifteen. In monkey years, the same age as Emily.

When Martyn was born in 1875, Emily was four. That was the year Emily met 'Drummie (Martyn), her invisible boy. One-hundred-years later, in 1975, Jon was four, the birthday when he received a toy paddle-steamer with its Steamboat Willie figure.

In 1981, when Jon was ten, he met is four-year-old girl ghost, named Click; I was also four.

In 1912, when Emily was forty-one, she first read *The Life Everlasting*; one-hundred-years later, in 2012, when Jon was forty-one, Emily asked him to read the same book.

In 1899, when Emily was twenty-seven, she met Martyn. One-hundred years later, in 1999, Jon is twenty-seven. I met Jon when I was twenty-seven. Records confirmed, that in the century markers 1900 and 2000, Emily and Jon were twenty-seven-years-old. I was fifteen.

In 1928, the cartoon 'Steamboat Willie' debuts; Emily is fifty-seven, the same year my father was born. Fifty-seven years later, I was born. Regina Watson was fifty-seven at the time of her death

Martyn died in 1972, the same year as Regina Watson.

In 1989, when I first encountered the monkey spirit Marmie 2, I was four-years-old.

In 1995, Marmie disappeared. I was ten. Jon was twenty-four, investigating the ghost of a mother named Margaret Marsh (the full name of Marmee in *Little Women*) Margaret told Jon she died in a

'Woo Woo VERONICA KNOX

'car' accident, with her four-year-old son. She was twenty-seven at the time. Her son's name was John with an 'h'.

Click, Jon's childhood ghost companion, died in 1945, the same year Emily died.

The group that Emily thought was holding her back, was the 'Group of Seven', not her sisters. Miss Emily Carr – was born in the same street she died, a few blocks apart.

And as for the apparition, 'Click'? Turns out, her name was a ten-year-old's interpretation of a four-year-old girl's pronunciation of the name 'Klee Wyck'.

Then something else *'clicked':* love remains hand-fast across the threshold of time, and life's synchronistic events evolve in full-circles linked as a chain. In old-age one can recall childhood as if it were yesterday and feel like a teenager or a twenty year-old or in the prime of maturity. Glass mirrors only distort the local images of our immortality into temporal waking nightmares.

TIME is a daydream of Maya inside the sleeping mind. Enjoy the present and start again at any TIME because even the illusion of death can make the heart grow stronger, and what better place could there be to start anew than in the past?

Timeline

1863 Richard Carr and his wife Emily Saunders
Carr arrive in Victoria.

1871 December 13 Emily Carr is born.

1876 William (Martyn) Paddon is born.

1875 Emily's brother Richard is born.

1886 Emily's mother dies. Emily is fifteen.

1888 Emily's father dies. Emily is seventeen.

1890-

1893 Attends the California School of Design in
San Francisco.

1899 Emily is twenty-seven. Meets William Mayo
Paddon aboard the steamship Willipa, in the
Spring.
Receives the nickname Klee Wyck, "the
laughing one," from the First Nations com-
munity in Ucluelet, British Columbia.
Travels to London to study at the Westmin-
ster School of Art.
Emily's brother Richard dies in California.

1900 Martyn visits London.
Emily refuses his numerous proposals of
marriage.

1901 Spends the winter in an artists colony in St.
Ives, Cornwall.

1903 Suffers a breakdown diagnosed as hysteria.
Remains in a sanatorium for eighteen months.

1904 Returns to Canada in June.

1910 Journeys to France to study art.
Enters an infirmary for eighteen months.

1911 Released from the infirmary in January.

WooWoo   VERONICA KNOX

1913 Suffers a second breakdown.
Returns to Victoria, builds Hill House, a four-suite apartment house on her share of her family's estate and becomes a landlord.

1919 Sisters Edith and Clara die.

1927 Meets members of the Canadian 'Group of Seven'.

1930 Exhibits with the 'Group of Seven'.
Meets Georgia O'Keeffe.

1933 Purchases 'the Elephant'.
Becomes an honorary member of the 'Group of Seven'.

1936 Sister Lizzie dies.

1937 Suffers first heart attack.

1939 Suffers second heart attack.

1942 Suffers third heart attack.

1944 Receives last Christmas love-letter from Martyn.

1945 Emily dies in March, age seventy-four.
Survived by sister Alice.

1972 William (Martyn) Paddon dies in California, age ninety-six.

Acknowledgements

Novels may be written in a vacuum, but they require a team of supporters to launch them into publication. I must first thank the support team of two professional women whom I have had the good fortunate to meet: my book designer, Iryna, from Spica Book Designs, and Linda Clement, my editor. Without these two amazing women, I would be the meek owner of a couple of dusty manuscripts in a drawer.

I thank Miss Emily Carr, that was. Obviously, her work and her commitment to art is a great legacy, but I would like to recognize the Emily who dedicated her care to so many creatures. Would that more humans were as compassionate as she.

I also wrote this in homage to Martyn (William Mayo Paddon) - Emily's steadfast beau, who carried the brunt of her dismissal and never faltered in his affections, sending Emily a flower each Christmas with his loving thoughts.

Author Ian McEwan's wonderful novel, *Atonement*, inspired me. McEwan's mastery gave nothing away, and so I was surprised and upset to learn at the end of the story that his fictional characters, Celia and Robby, had been separated by death, but I understood.

Fate is randomly cruel and kind, in predictably unpredictable ways. Happy endings can live or die on a single, fragile decision. A solid love-match is even more rare.

Fairy godmothers (human or simian) can do anything, including writing star-crossed lovers separated by death into a shamefully blissful finale, bestowing upon their characters a reprieve of love. We should all be so lucky.

About the Author

Veronica Knox lives on Vancouver Island with a menagerie of rescue pets. She still maintains it was she who had needed rescuing.

Veronica studied graphic design and illustration in the U.K. and has a Fine Arts Degree from the University of Alberta, where she studied Painting, Art History, and Classical Studies.

When she was four, she was bitten by a chimpanzee at the London Zoo. She has owned one and a half Old English Sheepdogs. She is absolutely mad for elephants, and she truly loathes any form of camping.

www.veronicaknox.com
www.woowoothenovel.com
contact email: veronica@veronicaknox.com